"I'm going to stay in the barn all night to make sure he's okay."

When Carter opened the door to the small office the strong smell of bitter coffee wafted out. "Want a cup?"

"Sure." Shannon followed him into the small room.

"Fair warning." He pulled two mugs from a deep drawer. "It's the leaded stuff."

"Good." Shannon accepted the cup of coffee from Carter. "Someone has to keep you awake."

He set his mug down and cocked his head. "You don't have to do that, you know. I'll be fine on my own. I can drink the whole pot. I won't let anything happen to Tater Tot, if that's what you're worried about."

After the pangs of loneliness Shannon had felt around her family earlier, she didn't want to head back to her bunkhouse. All that waited for her there were more reminders that she was alone and might always be. She wanted Carter's company right now.

Maybe she needed it.

And maybe—just maybe—he needed her company, too.

Even if he wasn't willing to admit it.

Avid reader, coffee drinker and chocolate aficionado **Jessica Keller** has degrees in communications and biblical studies and spends too much time on Instagram and Pinterest. Jessica calls the Midwest home. She lives for fall, farmers' markets and driving with the windows down. To learn more, visit Jessica at www.jessicakellerbooks.com.

Books by Jessica Keller

Love Inspired

Red Dog Ranch

The Rancher's Legacy
His Unexpected Return
The Wrangler's Last Chance

Goose Harbor

The Widower's Second Chance
The Fireman's Secret
The Single Dad Next Door
Small-Town Girl
Apple Orchard Bride
The Single Mom's Second Chance

Lone Star Cowboy League: Boys Ranch

The Ranger's Texas Proposal

Home for Good

Visit the Author Profile page at Harlequin.com for more titles.

The Wrangler's Last Chance

Jessica Keller

LOVE INSPIRED

INSPIRATIONAL ROMANCE

LOVE INSPIRED®
INSPIRATIONAL ROMANCE

Recycling programs
for this product may
not exist in your area.

ISBN-13: 978-1-335-48795-7

The Wrangler's Last Chance

This edition published by arrangement with Harlequin Books S.A.

For questions and comments about the quality of this book,
please contact us at CustomerService@Harlequin.com.

Love Inspired
22 Adelaide St. West, 40th Floor
Toronto, Ontario M5H 4E3, Canada
www.Harlequin.com

Printed in U.S.A.

But thou, O Lord, art a shield for me;
my glory, and the lifter up of mine head.
—*Psalm* 3:3

For Krista,
who patiently answered all my horse questions,
and for introducing the word *shrapnel* into my
daily vocabulary twenty years ago. But this still
doesn't mean I've forgotten that you laughed
at me when Serasity bucked me off.

Chapter One

Wing Crosby wasn't breathing.

Shannon Jarrett had charged into the water and scooped out her beloved pet goose when she spotted him floating upside down in the small pond in front of the staff bunkhouses at Red Dog Ranch. Now she dropped to her knees on the damp ground and ran her fingers down the goose's body. His little white-feathered head lolled to the side. His normally bright blue gaze was completely lidded.

"No. Wing. Please, don't do this." Her fingers trembled as she tried to feel for a heartbeat near his keel bone, but her fingers were shaking too much. She couldn't feel anything.

"Please don't die." She croaked out the words. "I can't lose you."

Not Wing. Not the little goose she had raised.

Please don't take him.

After everything she had been through the past year,

she couldn't stand another loss. She wasn't certain she could survive another heartbreak.

Hot tears blinded her for a second.

Was it possible to perform CPR on a goose? She knew their bones were different, hollow. If his heart wasn't beating, could she give him chest compressions without shattering his sternum? She had no idea. Maybe she would make things far worse.

Yet another situation in her life she would handle entirely wrong.

She had collected a lot of those lately.

A shiver rattled through her body. Being sopping wet at the end of March was a bad idea, even in Texas. But being cold was the least of her worries right now.

Move. Do something. Save him.

Blinking fiercely, she scanned the large ranch where most of her family lived. The ranch house was too far from where she was. Even if her eldest brother, Rhett, was inside, she would never make it to him in time. Not that he would necessarily know what to do anyway; he loved the dogs that hunted waterfowl, not the birds. Her brother Wade and his new wife, Cassidy, lived with their young daughter even farther across the ranch in the house they had recently finished building. Despite the fact that Wade only ever referred to Wing as Thanksgiving Dinner, she knew her twin brother would never hesitate to help her.

But there was no time.

In her haste, she had left her phone in her bunkhouse, or else she would have run a quick search on the internet for ideas. She had nothing. Nothing but the small body of her favorite little buddy dripping in her hands. He was dependent on her for his life and she was failing him.

A door slammed nearby and Shannon whirled to see who it was. Two doors down from the bunkhouse she called home, a tall man carried a bag into a staff house that had been empty for most of the last year. He had to be the head wrangler Rhett had recently hired. Shannon hadn't met him yet and didn't know anything about him, but at the moment he was her only hope.

Cradling Wing Crosby, Shannon rose and ran in the man's direction. "Help! Please. Help me."

He dropped the bag and jogged toward her.

"My goose. I need help." Shannon held out Wing Crosby. "I don't think he's breathing." Her voice broke. "I don't know what to do."

The man's electric-blue eyes latched onto hers. He nodded once and ripped off the coat he was wearing. He wrapped the fabric around Wing Crosby's body before gingerly lifting the goose from her arms and then he dropped to a knee, Wing Crosby in his lap. Opening up the jacket, he pressed his ear to Wing's chest.

"Not breathing, but there's a heartbeat." He squinted. "It's faint, but it's there." With a great amount of gentleness, the man opened Wing Crosby's beak and swept the inside of the goose's mouth with one of his fingers. "Did you see him choking on anything, or were you feeding him something when this happened?" The man kept his attention on Wing Crosby while he asked the question. His fingers combed over the bird's white feathers for injuries.

"I don't know what happened." Her voice took on a desperate tone. "I found him in the water. I didn't see anything."

He wrapped the jacket back around Wing and tucked the goose into the crook of his arm so the bird was snug against his body like a football. With his head tipped down, the man's dark hair fell across his forehead. The stranger rolled his shoulders as he took a deep breath.

Shannon dropped down in front of him so their knees touched. She just wanted to be by Wing. "You know what you're doing?"

The man glanced her way, the intensity of his blue eyes startling her again. He cocked an eyebrow. "You want me to save him, right?"

"Of course."

He nodded and focused his attention back on the goose. He wrapped a finger over the holes in Wing Crosby's bill, then put his mouth over the goose's bill and blew into the bird's mouth five times.

The man repeated the process three times before letting out a frustrated growl. "We've lost his heartbeat."

"Wait." Shannon laid a hand on the man's arm. "He's dead? Are you saying he's dead?" Her voice pitched up.

A muscle in the man's firm jaw ticked. "Not on my watch." He tugged open the jacket. Using three fingers, he pressed down on Wing's chest rapidly ten times. He followed that with five breaths and kept switching back and forth.

"I've had him since he hatched." Tears slipped down Shannon's cheek as she watched Wing being worked on.

"He's not even a year old yet, but he's really important to me," she said. "I can't lose him."

She had lost too much.

Too soon.

They had just passed the one-year anniversary of her father's sudden death, and hitting that first milestone had left her feeling raw all over again. He had been hit by a car; the driver had been focused on their phone instead of the man in the crosswalk. But that wasn't the only thing weighing her down. Her mother's Alzheimer's kept advancing, so every day it felt as if she was losing her all over again. Rhett had returned to the ranch exactly a year ago to claim his inheritance, but he had married right away and taken over the ranch house, which meant Shannon had been moved to a staff bunkhouse where she was living alone for the first time in her life. Her twin brother, Wade, who had been assumed dead for five years, had returned to the ranch last summer. Which was positive, but it had still been traumatic coming to terms with his betrayal, the fact he was still alive and forgiving him for letting them believe otherwise, only to find out he had cancer and they could lose him all over again. While Wade was considered cancer-free now, there was always a chance it could return. Being his sole support during that time had been stressful.

And then there had been Cord.

Who had gifted her the negative track of thoughts that played on repeat in her mind.

The boyfriend who had left bruises on her arms.

Scars on her heart.

At least the experience with Cord had broken Shannon of her childish daydreams about relationships and love. There wasn't a perfect someone out there waiting for her. Maybe for others—people like her brothers and their wives—but not for her. She needed to pick herself up, be strong on her own and figure out what a life without anyone else in it looked like.

Because despite how much she loved being around people, loved connecting and had always wanted a family, *alone* might be what God had for her.

And she was determined to be okay with that.

No matter how much it hurt.

While breaking free of Cord had ultimately been a good thing, it had sent her world reeling. With her brothers busy in their new marriages and her mother no longer capable of being her confidante, Shannon had been entirely left out and alone. The only thing that had gotten her through the worst of it had been raising the little abandoned goose, because he had been completely dependent on her for survival. He had given her something to focus on.

He had needed her when no one else had. He had nestled up to her and gazed at her adoringly when her family had treated her as if she was weak, as if they expected her to fall apart. Whenever their eyes met hers, the pity they held was too clear to stomach.

For once she just wanted them to see her as strong. She wanted a reason for them to be proud of her. She would give anything to be seen as more in their eyes than the little sister they all had to watch out for, to constantly protect.

All of a sudden, Wing made a horrible half honk,

half gasping sound and his whole body trembled. In one swift motion the man set the goose down, grabbed Shannon's arm and hauled her to her feet a few steps away.

"If you're right in their face sometimes they'll bite when they come to," he said. His gaze fell to where he gripped her arm and he immediately let go of her. "Even people they know. Their body goes into a mode. Thinking something is latched onto them—that's usually the behavior of a predator, not someone trying to save them." He shoved a hand into his almost black hair and let out a long, loud breath. "And geese have shockingly painful bites." His laugh was soft and self-conscious.

Wing Crosby's eye blinked open and drooped shut, then flew open again. The goose tried to lift his head but set it back down again. He opened his bill and wheezed a few times.

He was alive.

Shannon squealed and threw her arms around the man. "You saved him. I don't know how to thank you. I can't believe you were able to save him." She hugged him tightly. He was so much taller than her. His chest was solid, his shoulders wide, and he smelled of something delightfully spicy. She was breathing deeply when she realized he wasn't hugging back.

In fact, upon contact, the man's body had gone completely rigid.

Shannon was so used to the freedom of hugging her brothers, she hadn't stopped to think before tossing herself at the poor guy. Then again, she never nuzzled for extra whiffs of her brothers, either.

She extricated her arms from around his torso. "Sorry."

"No problem." His lips tilted into something that looked like it wanted to be a smile when it grew up. He scooped his coat off the ground and offered it to her. "You've been shuddering the whole time. It's a little wet from him, but it'll be better than nothing. I'm guessing I won't be able to convince you to leave him to go change."

Wing gave a loud snuffle as he finally sat up.

Shannon slipped on the man's coat right before she picked up Wing.

The man leaned closer to the goose. "I'd call your vet and get him looked at. They often need to be intubated after something like this." He tentatively petted Wing's head. "You've got a beautiful bird there. Looks like a pilgrim gander."

So not only did the man know his goose breeds, but the correct term for a male goose, as well. Not to mention knowing how to do CPR on one.

She opened her mouth to say something but wasn't quite sure where to start.

"He needs to be warmed up while you wait for the doctor," the man continued. "If you have a heating pad they work great. Just put a towel over it and put it in a carrier so he's contained and on top of the warmth source. You'll want to minimize any stress for him."

"I will." Shannon offered him a smile. "I'm Shannon, by the way." And between charging into the pond and crying, she probably looked a wreck, but thankfully, the man was treating her as if this had all been a normal, everyday interaction.

"Carter Kelly. New head wrangler." He thumbed toward the large barn situated at the front of the property.

"And apparently goose saver," Shannon said. "I don't know how to thank you."

He shook his head. "Don't mention it. It was nothing. Seriously."

Shannon hadn't been paying much attention to the man's looks while she was worried about Wing Crosby, but now that she was looking at Carter he was hard to glance away from. Dark, almost black hair and blue eyes that matched Wing Crosby's. In his boots, jeans and white T-shirt, Carter Kelly could have been the image that popped up on an internet search titled World's Handsomest Cowboy. A few jagged scars along his neck and jawline only added to his appeal.

"You should call the vet," Carter repeated.

His voice snapped her back to normal behavior. First she had hugged the guy and now she was very obviously gawking at him. Great first impression.

Shannon nodded and stepped backward. Her arms tightened around Wing Crosby as he tucked his head onto her shoulder. "I'm going to. Right now." She took another step back. "What are you going to do?"

"Me?" Carter chuckled. "Probably go gargle antibacterial hand soap a few times. Birds are germ magnets." He shrugged. "Then finish unpacking." He pointed at her as he backed away. "But let me know what the doc says, okay?"

"I will," she said and then rushed Wing Crosby into her bunkhouse to warm him up, change into something dry and wait for Dr. Spira to arrive. While she waited, she tried to think of an appropriate way to thank Carter Kelly. The man had saved her pet. She had to do *something* to thank him.

Seeing his blue eyes and chiseled jaw again had nothing to do with it.

It didn't.

Because Shannon Jarrett was done with men.

For now, certainly, but maybe for good, as well.

"Well, except for you, of course." Shannon patted Wing's head and he honked quietly from his perch on the blanket-covered heating pad. His eyes closed again.

She no longer trusted her heart when it came to these things, so the fact that she found Carter attractive meant nothing. Her heart only ever got her into trouble. So it had been demoted. Every choice from here on would be logical. Thought through. No emotions. No heartache.

But it was logical to thank someone.

Living a life without roots meant Carter Kelly had never owned much, but the generous bunkhouse he had been given as one of the perks of his new job at Red Dog Ranch dwarfed his meager possessions even more than usual. It was almost embarrassing, but it would be the biggest place he had lived in since his stepdad had tossed him out on his ear all those years ago. At least the place had come furnished. If it hadn't, his new home would have looked really pathetic with nothing in it.

Not *new* home.

Temporary.

Temporary home.

He couldn't afford to think of places as his or grow attached to anything. It wasn't his style. Getting attached meant getting involved, meant hurting when he left or was told to move along. It meant missing and longing for a place and people who probably wouldn't think about him after he was gone.

No, thank you.

Going down that road once had been enough for him. He would work here a year or two, tops. Pay down some of his school debt while he enjoyed the free room and board and then move on to get experience elsewhere. Carter would gather as many different learning experiences as he could. If he stayed on course, he could one day achieve his dream of saving enough to begin his own practice. Then when people and animals were solely dependent on him, he would be prepared. He wouldn't let any of them down or fail them.

It was a solid plan. The perfect plan.

One that had worked for him countless times before.

One that had kept him safe.

Still, he thanked God for at least the twentieth time that day for providing him this job at Red Dog Ranch. Nowhere else he had applied to had offered room and board along with a decent salary. Some offered a place to stay but charged a small rent. Not to mention the fact that the other prospective employers had all asked probing questions about why he would want to work grunt jobs for them when he had a DVM degree.

You're a doctor, son. Why would you waste that here at my farm?

Of course I could use a veterinarian on staff, but I don't have the money for one and this is a lowly position at a pig farm, so I have to ask myself what you're trying to pull here.

But his new boss hadn't seemed all that concerned or impressed with Carter's credentials. All Rhett Jarrett had wanted to know was what experience he had with horses, what leadership roles he'd been in before and who his references were. So many years spent working any job he could find at the ranches that dotted both the West and Midwest had paid off. Rhett had been impressed with his horsemanship and the quality of the ranches Carter had worked at.

Carter flipped a switch and can lights nestled across the ceiling buzzed to life.

He had thought about touring the ranch after he finished unpacking, but with it still being only early spring, evening had draped the area quicker than he had anticipated. He would save his exploring for tomorrow.

Sighing, Carter tugged the folder full of his loan paperwork from his backpack and tossed it onto the kitchen table. When it landed, the folder slid a bit. A small dog-eared notecard peeked out the edge. He picked it up and ran his thumb over the Bible verse he had written there. *But Thou, O Lord, art a shield for me; my glory, and the lifter up of mine head.* He had carried this for twelve years. Ever since Audrey.

Most of the time, Carter put a lot of effort into *not*

thinking about Audrey, but a reminder as he started at a new place wasn't a bad thing.

A warning to be careful—not to let his guard down with anyone—no matter how much his extrovertly wired brain begged him to connect with others. Connecting only ever got him burned.

Audrey was his cautionary tale.

A lesson he never needed to learn again.

So why had he told the woman today—Shannon—to keep him updated on the gander?

Carter scrubbed his hand over his face and shot out a long stream of air.

He was a veterinarian who had performed a procedure on an animal and he wanted to see if he had done the right thing, learn if there was something else he could have done in the situation. Grow as a professional and be better prepared for the future he one day hoped to have. That was all.

The fact that Shannon was beautiful wouldn't—couldn't—factor in. Though with her short, wavy blond hair, curvy frame and wide eyes, she was impossible not to acknowledge. Even dripping water from a pond overrun with algae, she had caused him to be flustered for a moment there.

He tucked the verse card back into the file.

He ruined people's lives when he got involved.

He was a liability and always would be.

Someone knocked on the door and Carter rushed to answer it. Even though he wasn't set to officially start working until Monday, maybe his new boss wanted him to take care of something today.

He opened the door to find Shannon smiling beside a bald, hunched-over man with age spots peppering his face and hands. She held a teal-colored plateful of what might have been cupcakes. They were certainly baked in cupcake wrappers, but whatever frosting there had once been had melted and pooled onto the plate in a shiny puddle.

Shannon grimaced. "These were supposed to be a thank-you." She glanced down at the plate. "I'm not the best cook. Not like Cassidy—she's our head chef, and these would make her faint." Shannon pressed the plate toward him. "They're just from a box and I think— okay, I *know* I didn't wait long enough before frosting them but…" She lifted one shoulder in a half shrug.

Frosting sloshed onto Carter's thumb when he took the plate. He looked down at the offering and his chest felt tight. He swallowed hard. "You made me cupcakes?"

"Well, sort of." Her laugh was quiet, a little nervous. "I wanted to do something nice for you but you totally have my permission to throw them away when I'm not looking. I probably should have just picked you up something from the bakery in town tomorrow." She reached to take the plate back. "In fact, let's do that. Let's pretend you never saw these and I can just toss them myself."

He protectively moved the plate to his side, away from her so she couldn't reach them. "No, it's not… I, ah—" Carter cleared his throat. *Get it together, man.* Baked goods weren't supposed to make a person emotional. He swallowed once, twice. "It's just no one's ever made something for me before. Thank you. I want to keep them."

Shannon tilted her head. "I find that hard to believe." She rolled her hand. "I mean, someone at some point has baked you cookies. That's pretty standard. Your family or—" her eyes narrowed as she assessed him "—I'd guess a girlfriend."

No, but his last girlfriend had called him trash. Did that count for bonus points?

He shook his head. He had already been too vulnerable and he needed to reel the situation back to somewhere comfortable for him. Carter motioned for them to follow him into the bunkhouse. With great care, he set the plate of cupcakes on his table.

The older gentleman braced his hands on the other side of the table. "That was some fine work you did on Wing Crosby, if I do say so myself. You've got some great instincts."

"Wing Crosby?" Carter looked between them for an explanation.

"My goose." Shannon frowned. "Well, I guess if I'm talking to animal people I can call him a gander." Then she added, "I like old movies."

"I'm going to bring him back to my clinic to monitor him overnight, but he looks great. Your quick thinking definitely saved our little friend." The other man held out his hand. "I'm Dr. Spira."

Carter shook the man's hand and gave him his name.

Dr. Spira held on to his hand. "Shannon said you were a natural with Wing. Seems to me as if you've had some advanced training, given the instructions you gave her afterward."

There was no reason for Carter to withhold the truth. His degrees had been clearly labeled on his résumé when he applied to Red Dog Ranch.

"I have my DVM," Carter confirmed.

"Ah." The doctor nodded. "So you're Dr. Kelly, then. Well, meeting you is my pleasure."

"I'm not practicing right now," he explained as if that mattered. To him it did. "Just Carter."

"DVM." Shannon's brow scrunched. "I feel as if I'm at some elite convention where everyone talks in codes and I'm automatically supposed to know what you're saying. The force be with you, and all that. And that's cool, but can someone please translate for me here?"

Dr. Spira turned toward her, his smile warm and fatherly. "Doctor of veterinary medicine."

"Wait." She whirled toward Carter. "You're a vet?"

He shrugged. "I could be. But not right now. Today I'm a head wrangler."

Dr. Spira grabbed Carter's shoulder and gave it a squeeze. "It'll be nice to talk to someone with fresh training. I'm the only one local and don't get too many meetups anymore. Do you mind if I come and consult with you from time to time when I'm at the ranch? My office is in town, but I'm here often enough."

Thankfulness surged through Carter's chest again. Learn from someone who had years and years in the field with no catch involved? He wanted to hug the man, but he refrained. However, he was certain his excitement was plain in his voice when he said, "Not at all. I'd love that, actually." It was more than Carter had ever dreamed of when he accepted the position at Red Dog Ranch.

Dr. Spira excused himself but Shannon stayed in his bunkhouse. She crossed her arms and studied Carter.

Carter raised an eyebrow. "Still trying to take back those cupcakes?"

She pursed her lips. "I'm trying to figure you out."

His laugh held an undercurrent of nerves he hoped she didn't pick up on. "I'm afraid there isn't much to figure out." He lifted his hands at his sides in an exaggerated manner. "Just a simple man trying to make an honest living."

Her eyes narrowed and for some reason that made her even more adorable. "Does my brother know you're a vet?"

"Your brother?"

Shannon huffed. "Rhett."

"Rhett Jarrett is your brother?" The information landed in his mind like a punch. Would he always be attracted to the wrong women? At least these days he knew not to act on attraction. Or because a woman had done something nice for him, like bake him cupcakes. Just because he was starved for kindness, he couldn't read more into such gestures than what they were— neighborly behavior that most of the world probably wrote off as simple, everyday occurrences.

She tapped her chin. "That *would* explain why my last name is also Jarrett."

"But I saw you head into one of the staff houses."

"It's a long story." She sighed. "But the quick version

is my brother owns the ranch, so he and his wife live in the big house and don't exactly need me wandering around there while they're living their newlywed life."

"He knows." Carter brought the conversation away from the dangerous territory of getting to know someone more than was absolutely necessary. "I didn't hide anything from him. If that's what you're asking."

"Oh, settle down." She held up her hands. "I wasn't accusing you of anything. If you have an asset that could be useful to the ranch I only wanted to make sure Rhett knew." Shannon glanced around his bunkhouse. "Well, I'm sure you want to relax after moving in, so I'll leave you to it. But I'll see you around, okay?"

Carter walked her to the door to see her out. He leaned around her to open the front door and caught the scents of vanilla or caramel or something equally sweet. Probably from baking. But she had showered and changed since their earlier run-in and she was even more beautiful than she had been then. Her large brown eyes held his for a moment and he sucked in a sharp breath.

He pulled back, leaving as much distance as possible as he opened the door for her. He stood in the doorway as she walked two doors down to her home, the whole time telling himself to go back inside, to look away. But she had been the first person to hug him in years and he just wanted to make sure she got home safely. That was it.

Because Shannon Jarrett was off-limits.

She was his boss's sister.

Another life he would destroy if he allowed himself to get involved.

Which he wouldn't. He never did. Not since Audrey.

He would keep his head down. Do his job. Learn what he could from Dr. Spira, then hightail it out of Texas. Run to a place where no one knew him and start over from scratch like he always did.

But first he would have a cupcake.

Chapter Two

Shannon ran a currycomb in a circular motion over the bay gelding named Memphis. Memphis was a large but gentle and patient horse, which made the big lug perfect for the Mighty Girls Horse Lessons Rhett had placed Shannon in charge of for the spring session. Girls from the area who were in the foster care system were offered the opportunity to learn how to ride and take care of horses for free at Red Dog Ranch. The winter session had been canceled, but they hadn't wanted to do that again. Her father had been gone a year and it was high time for all the programs to be up and running as usual again.

While the Jarrett family homestead was a working cattle ranch, the main mission of Red Dog Ranch was to serve to better the lives of foster children. The ranch ran a free summer camp program, hosted holiday parties, had internships available to teenagers who wanted experience for their résumés and had programmed classes and lessons throughout the year, like the riding lessons, among other things. Rhett and his wife, Macy, had recently gone through the process of being approved to be foster parents, as well. Everyone who lived on the property was busy and many were overextended at the moment.

Mighty Girls Horse Lessons was usually run by one of the staff members, but there had been so many changes at the ranch in the course of the last year that the staff was still in flux and Rhett had been at a loss, which was how the lessons had ended up on Shannon's plate. Not that she minded. It was nice to be in charge of something, even if it was temporary.

Even if she had been his last pick.

She was surprised he wasn't here to hover over her. Like he usually did.

Since the breakup with Cord, Rhett and Wade had both engaged in far too much hovering. As if Shannon might fall apart if they weren't around to take care of her. At first she hadn't minded—it had almost been sweet—but now it was nothing short of annoying. She knew they had watched over her these last nine months because they loved her and wanted only the best for her. And whenever she got frustrated, she reminded herself how blessed she was to have a family that cared so much, but it was high time they let her be.

Allowed her to sink or swim on her own.

Between Cord's controlling ways and now her brothers' overprotection, she was so sick of men calling the shots in her life. She wished someone would come alongside her and cheer her on or join what she was doing instead of telling her what to do.

Was it so bad to want her brothers to see her as something other than their baby sister? Once, just once, she would love it if they had admiration in their eyes, pride instead of pity.

Because either her dad or brothers had always stepped up to run things, Shannon had never actually been in charge of anything at the ranch before. In high school she had been happy to serve as a summer camp counselor at the ranch, and as she had gotten older, she had started floating around the ranch, pitching in wherever necessary but never having a defined role. A fact that had never bothered her before, not as long as she was busy and felt useful. But now she questioned why she hadn't asked her father for more responsibility and opportunities to lead when there had been chances. The way her life had panned out, she knew a little about a lot of aspects at the ranch, but she was a master of nothing. She wished it was different, but wishes never helped anything.

Shannon gripped the brush a little harder. She would change all that now. She would square her shoulders and swallow her doubts and learn how to lead.

Rhett had told her the new head wrangler would be aiding her with the lessons, and for that Shannon was grateful. While she didn't want one of her brothers nosing around, she didn't mind the newcomer. He didn't know her past, her failures. For all he knew she was capable and smart. A strong woman.

Far from the truth.

Finished with the currycomb, Shannon traded it out for a large stiff brush that she used in a sweeping motion to clear the dirt and hair the currycomb had loosened. She sighed. If only it was as easy to brush away her mistakes and worries. In a show of affection, Memphis leaned into her. There was a reason he was one of Shannon's favorites among all their trail horses.

In nearby stalls Carter and Easton, a teenage boy who'd started volunteering at Red Dog Ranch a few months ago, were both busy getting other horses ready for riders. There were only six girls in the class this session, so they had two horses apiece to prepare.

"How long are these lessons?" Easton's words from one stall over made her jump.

"Forty-five minutes. We'll do fifteen minutes of review to make sure they remember everything from the last session since it's been a few months, and five minutes of instruction for the emergency dismount. Then they'll have twenty minutes to practice and work with their horses before cleanup," Shannon answered.

Carter came up to Memphis's stall door and leaned his forearms across the top of it. "Emergency dismount? That's tough stuff for new riders." He tilted his head. "How old did you say these girls were?" Last night Shannon had considered him attractive, but today he was even more appealing in his cowboy hat.

She fumbled with the brush in her hand. Memphis snorted.

Appealing was dangerous. She would do well to remember that.

She sucked in a sharp breath. The scents of straw and dust and dirt reminded her of what was important.

The kids the ranch served. The ranch itself. Making her brothers proud again and carrying on her father's legacy.

"These girls are intermediate-level riders," she said. "They've already passed our other courses." She rested a hand on Memphis's side. "And hopefully, they'll never need to perform an emergency dismount, but I'd rather have them know how to do it than get into a dangerous situation on a horse someday and not know how to handle themselves."

"Makes sense." Carter nodded as he straightened. "This is your gig. I trust your judgment."

He probably wouldn't have said that if he knew her. Still, it was nice to hear.

She forced a smile as she checked her watch. "Ten minutes until they arrive." She peeked at Easton through the slats between the stalls. The redheaded teenager wore a baggy T-shirt over his thin frame. "Tell me you brought a coat this time? It's cold out there." Cooler than March in Texas normally was.

Easton shrugged. "It's not so bad."

Shannon's heart twisted and she fought the urge to go into the next stall and hug the boy. Or shake some sense into him. But Easton had been in and out of foster care his entire life, so she knew he had little in the way of possessions and was often not dressed for the weather. They did so much to help kids like Easton at Red Dog Ranch but there were always more needs than resources.

She tugged keys out of her jeans and tossed them to Carter, who impressively caught them one-handed. "Check the office at the front of the barn. My brothers are forever leaving coats in there."

Carter held the keys up by the keychain that was shaped like a rose. "Your brother gave me keys to the barn office, too. I work here, you know."

Right. Her cheeks warmed. Carter wasn't one of the teen volunteers she had grown used to working along-side in the past year; he was the head wrangler. A paid staff member. Any more, the barn office would be more his domain than hers. She held out her hand, taking the keys back with a small apologetic half smile.

As Carter turned to go, Shannon traced her fingers through the soft hairs on Memphis's neck. He nickered. She sighed and rested her forehead on his shoulder for a second. She loved working with the girls and didn't mind teaching lessons but she couldn't help feeling as if something was missing from her life. The lessons would only last for a few weeks, and then, after that, what would she do? Lately, because they had been short on staff and she had always enjoyed working with the animals, she had been helping to take care of the horses and doing chores around the barn, but with a new head wrangler she would no longer be needed as much here, either. She would go back to floating around the ranch doing odd jobs.

No set place. No set path.

Rhett owned the place and was the director. His pregnant wife, Macy, was a codirector and she man-aged the ranch's office and administrative affairs. Shan-non's twin, Wade, had recently taken over the position of head of maintenance, and his new wife, Cassidy, was the head chef. They all had defined roles. Purposes. The ranch would cease to function without any of them.

But if Shannon up and left she wouldn't be missed. The ranch would continue on just fine.

For the first time in her life, Shannon wasn't sure she belonged at Red Dog Ranch.

A pit formed in her stomach. She wasn't needed.

A text made her phone buzz in her back pocket. She slipped her phone out to see a message from Wade: Cassidy and I have to run out. When you go to get Thanksgiving Dinner make sure Rhett goes with you.

She rolled her eyes at Wade's name for Wing Crosby and was trying to think of something clever to text back when the barn doors slammed open and six ten-year-old girls rushed in.

For now, in this space, she was needed. She would pour herself into these girls and send them back to their homes full of praise and encouragement and the knowledge that people at Red Dog Ranch cared about them.

Afterward she would have plenty of time to figure out where and if she still belonged here.

Carter stood in the center of the corral and turned in a slow circle, trying to keep an eye on all the riders as they practiced their emergency dismounts. Clouds plodded through the sky like a herd of lazy cattle, but even then, it was much nicer out than he was used to for the time of year. March in the Northern states still brought plenty of snowstorms and frozen ground, but here in Texas it was already sunny and green. He had to cover a smile when he heard Shannon insist that all the girls zip up their coats.

Shannon repositioned her horse so the kids could

get another look at how to perform the dismount. "The most important thing is to get your feet clear of the stirrups." She had told them they would only be practicing the dismount from a stopped position today but if they did well, then they could try it at a walk in the coming weeks. "Hands on the withers." She put her hands on the horse's neck. "Kick out of the stirrups, then jump, using the horse as a vault—really push away from him." She perfectly kicked her legs out and vaulted away from her horse, landing to the left. Done demonstrating, she handed the reins to Easton. "Really launch yourself away from your horse. Remember, if you're doing an emergency dismount it's a bad situation to begin with, so you're trying to get off and away."

Shannon stopped to give a struggling rider some extra attention, and within a few minutes she had the girl laughing and trying again. She caught Carter watching her and smiled as she crossed to where he stood. Her short blond curls bobbed with each step.

"Are you sure you're not cold?" Shannon jutted her chin toward him. As she stepped close he caught a whiff of the same vanilla-and-caramel smell that had lingered around her last night. So not just the cupcakes. Something she wore.

He swallowed hard.

Carter knew she was talking about his coat. When he hadn't found an extra in the office, he had shed his, giving it to Easton. At first the boy had protested, but when Carter had insisted, he'd relented easily enough.

"I'll be just fine." He realized that people who were used to the Texas weather might think it was cold out, but his Northern blood was feeling warm even in the jeans and button-down he had on. He should have just worn a T-shirt. He had been glad to shirk his unnecessary coat. Even gladder when the teenage boy had fawned over the article of clothing like it was the nicest thing he had ever worn. Carter would probably just tell Easton to keep it.

"I had wanted to have an indoor arena built last summer." She hooked her thumbs into her pockets and scraped the toe of her boot into the dirt. "That way we could ride in any type of weather and it would shield the horses and riders from the worst of the sun in the summer. It would have opened up the ranch to host more types of events, too."

"They're useful, but they can be expensive." He had helped build one when he had worked at Dove's Peak Ranch in Wyoming. But there they were sometimes hit with feet of snow, so the arena had been a much-needed addition to keep the horses exercised during the long winters.

"It had been on the list, but with the storm—" She met his gaze. "Did you know this place was almost leveled by a tornado a year ago?"

Carter took his time looking out over the expanse of Red Dog Ranch—large buildings, brand-new cabins and barns, fields of healthy grasses and a huge herd of cattle. "You guys have done an amazing job rebuilding." He noticed Shannon's frown. Carter cleared his throat. "But I'm guessing the indoor arena got scrapped from the build list after the storm?" And for some reason that really mattered to her. He wondered why. Maybe she just really loved horses.

"For a while it was still on, but everything else took priority, you know?" Her mouth twisted to the side. "So it just kept getting moved down the list until there weren't funds left. I tried to argue for it but I was over-ruled." She sighed. "I guess it doesn't matter."

His mind was stuck on *overruled*.

"By your brothers?" Rhett had explained to Carter how their father had passed unexpectedly last spring, leaving Rhett with the ranch. Now, from what Carter could tell so far, Rhett and Wade oversaw everything. But if Shannon was a Jarrett, then her opinion should matter, too.

She gave a quick laugh. "Yeah, all three of them. Even Boone, who doesn't even live here, outvoted me." She held up a hand. "But they were right. It was the least important item on the list. It would have been nice on a day like today, though. The girls are freezing." She rubbed her arms as if she might have been cold, too, despite the fitted jacket she had on. "And it would defi-nitely come in handy in the summer."

Carter folded his arms over his chest. He hadn't known there were three Jarrett brothers. All the more reason to give Shannon a wide berth. Carter didn't want to get caught in the crosshairs with any of the Jarretts.

Still, he fought the desire to press her about why the arena had been so important to her, but he swallowed that question. *Too personal. Stick to the weather.* "It's what—upper fifties out here?"

Shannon kept her eyes on the girl she had just been

helping. "It's a little colder than normal. Usually we start hitting the seventies by now." A couple of the kids even wore winter hats.

Carter chuckled. "Where I'm from this is called summer weather. We don't wear coats unless it's well below freezing."

Shannon turned to face him. Even in the diminished sunlight, her brown eyes held unreadable depths of both light and dark hues. "And where is that, where you're from? You haven't said."

He had walked right into that, hadn't he? Personal information he didn't want to give.

Carter shrugged. "North."

She didn't need to know about his sad upbringing in Montana or the many states he'd meandered through in the last thirteen years, either.

"That encompasses a lot of places." She arched an eyebrow. "But you know that, don't you, Doctor?"

Doctor.

The title still felt odd, like a child slipping into his dad's too-big shoes.

If you were going to spend all that time and waste so much money, I don't know why you couldn't have become a real doctor. That would have been something. But you threw that all away on animals. Too bad. It would have been nice to tell people my son was really a doctor.

Carter clenched his jaw as he shoved his father's words away. His dad's opinion had stopped mattering the day he had walked out on Carter and his mom to run off with his much younger mistress. Had mattered even less when he had turned Carter away when he had showed up at his front door as a homeless teenager.

I don't want you near your half siblings. You'll be a bad influence on them. I haven't even told them they have a big brother. They have bright futures and I don't need you ruining their lives.

Then his father had taken his new family and moved to California. Far enough to make sure Carter would never be a part of his stepbrothers' lives.

There was a reason he didn't dwell on the past.

He mentally shook his father's words away like a horse shaking off bothersome flies so he could focus on Shannon, who was smiling warmly, waiting for him to answer her.

"I've been a lot of places." There. Nonspecific and revealed nothing.

"How cryptic of you." Shannon popped her hand on her hip. "Work with me here, cowboy. At least name your favorite one." She blew a strand of hair away from her face. "Listen, I just want to hear about someplace other than here. I've been nowhere. Never left Texas. Pathetic, right?"

"It's an awfully big state," he offered.

"But I've always wanted to see other places. Be adventurous." She shrugged.

"Moving around, it's not all it's cracked up to be."

"Still, what was your favorite place?" she pressed. "I'd love to hear." Apparently Shannon was an expert at directing the conversation and was used to dealing with difficult men, because she wasn't about to let up.

The fine art of male question avoidance didn't seem to faze her whatsoever.

Oh, well. Talking about places he had lived in didn't have to be personal. "Montana is really something. The sky there," he said. "It doesn't compare to anywhere else. But Idaho has something special, too—something different. It's a sort of hidden gem." And if she asked Rhett, she would know he had studied at Colorado State University, so it didn't hurt to mention that state, either. "Then, of course, Colorado and the mountains are pretty inspiring."

She gave a low whistle. "Well, cowboy, you really have been everywhere."

"Not everywhere," he said. "The world's a big place and there's still a lot more to see. I'd like to mark it all off my list someday if I could." The last part had slipped out. More than he had wanted to share with her.

"That's as good a dream as any, I guess." Her smile was wistful. It made him want to ask what her dream was. He bit that question down right away.

She called to a girl named Susan. "Don't be afraid to grab the mane if you need to stabilize yourself before you jump, okay? It won't hurt your horse at all." They watched each of the girls try a few more times before Shannon told them that they could stop practicing their dismounts and ride a few laps to close out the session.

Carter came up beside her again. "Have you heard from Dr. Spira? About the goose?"

Her face lit up. "Wing had a great night. The vet said I could go pick him up this afternoon." She bounced a little. "I can't wait."

"That's great to hear." He was glad the little gander hadn't experienced any complications. It was nice to know he had done the right thing. Carter might have received his DVM but a piece of paper and a handful of years in school didn't mean he automatically knew everything there was to know about doctoring animals. That was where experience and further study came in.

Someday he would be confident enough in his abilities and knowledge to strike out alone. But not until he knew more. Not until he was certain he would always be able to help and make the right call. Right out of school he had worked at a clinic and made a mistake in a diagnosis that had cost a family their beloved pet. He never wanted that to happen again.

"Do you want to come with me into town?" Shannon's question surprised him. "To pick Wing up?" She rocked on the toes of her boots. "I'm sure Spira would love the chance to chat with you again."

While he did want more opportunities to get to know the local veterinarian, he didn't know if offering to go anywhere with his boss's sister was the best plan for his future. "No, you go. I'll take care of unsaddling the horses so you can head out right when the girls leave, if you want."

Her smile faded. "Right, okay, that works."

Shannon drifted toward the edge of the corral and unlatched the gate as she instructed the girls to bring their horses back to the barn to be unsaddled and brushed down. "Make sure you fill their buckets with fresh water before each of you leave."

Easton came up beside Carter. The tips of his ears

were red. "I can take care of unsaddling and feeding. This might be the first riding lesson, but I've been helping get the horses ready for the ranch hands for weeks now. You should go with her."

"Why?" Carter hadn't even known Easton had been close enough to hear their conversation.

"Her brothers won't let her go get him unless someone goes along." Easton slouched as he walked, his hands shoved deep into the pockets of the oversize coat. His posture made Carter's heart twist. He had been that boy before—scrawny and alone and hoping no one picked up on how sad he was. Carter didn't want to embarrass Easton by pressing him to reveal more about his situation than the teen boy was willing to, but he promised himself he would keep an eye on Easton and help him whenever he could. Care about him.

Something Carter wished someone had done for him at that age.

Easton rubbed at his nose. "She told me Wade's busy and I know Rhett's off ranch today, too. Before the lesson she asked me how long I was sticking around today, but my ride should be here sooner than it would take to go back and forth to town. If she asked me, then she's at her wit's end trying to find someone."

"Why don't her brothers let her go into town on her own?" Shannon was a grown woman who hardly needed her brothers' permission to do things. Unease swam through Carter's gut. In all his interactions with his new boss, Rhett had seemed like a stand-up guy. He really hoped his impression of the man was correct.

"Beats me." Easton shrugged. "I only started here a

few months ago and they've always been like that since I've been here. All I know is that Miss Shannon wants to get her goose and she'll catch heat from one or both of those Jarretts if she heads to town alone."

He's really important to me.

I can't lose him.

Shannon's frantic words from last night swam through Carter's mind.

Carter closed the gate once all the horses were on their way to the barn. He scrubbed his chin while he watched the retreating forms of Shannon and Easton. He had witnessed firsthand how much that goose meant to Shannon. And she had been nothing but kind to Carter in all their interactions so far. She didn't have to be nice to the new staff member. He was still touched by her gesture of making him cupcakes.

He lifted his hat to run a hand over his hair. What would it hurt? He could drive into town with her.

To get to know Dr. Spira better, of course.

And if the Jarrett brothers had a valid reason to be concerned for their sister's safety, Carter hardly wanted her decision to go alone pinned on his refusal. Getting on Rhett's bad side his first day on the job wasn't ideal. Carter rolled his shoulders. He could handle being around the sister of the person in charge without losing his head or heart.

It wouldn't be like last time.

Carter jogged toward the barn to catch her before she headed out alone.

Chapter Three

Carter gripped the leather-wrapped steering wheel as he turned his truck to drive out of Red Dog Ranch. His old pickup rattled a little as it ground its way over the pebbled driveway. He had purchased the thing used years ago and had brought the truck back to life more times than he could count. The hunk of metal had been with him longer than most of his possessions. And definitely longer than most people.

Shannon rested her elbow on the armrest between them. "Thanks for driving with me. What made you change your mind?"

Before he pulled out onto the road, Carter checked another time for coming cars. The speed limit was high on the road in front of Red Dog Ranch and his truck took a bit to get up to speed, so he had to wait for a large window or pocket of space to safely maneuver into. "You made a good point—it's a good chance to talk to Dr. Spira again. And I'm new here." He gave her a tilted grin. "I should probably start to get the lay of the land, right?"

She laughed softly. "Oh, that won't take long. Stillwater isn't a very impressive town." She directed him to turn left at the next road. A few minutes later they were driving down Hickory Lane.

"This is the main drag," Shannon explained.

Storefronts with colorful awnings dotted each side of the road—a bakery, a hardware store, a few mom-and-pop cafés and more than half a dozen small churches. He had seen towns like this before, lived in them and been burned by them. Small towns were dangerous because everyone knew everyone, and people talked and banded together. In places like this, boredom bred drama. If someone important decided they didn't like a person, then the whole town shunned them. Made them feel as unwelcome as they could.

At least, that had been Carter's small-town experience.

He pointed at a bright banner suspended above the road. It was festooned with fake flower chains and a large painted sun. "'Stillwater Spring Pageant. Bring your brightest smile to the brightest event of the year,'" he said, reading out loud. "Big-time stuff here."

"Hey." Shannon narrowed her eyes in a joking manner. "That *is* a big-deal thing around here. Little girls fight to be named the Stillwater Sunshine Princess."

"Did you ever enter?"

She tucked some of her hair behind her ear. He didn't miss the wash of red that dotted her cheeks. "I'm pleading the Fifth on that one."

Carter laughed. At least Shannon was fun to be around. She wasn't the type to be nervous or try to bat her eyes at a guy. Confidence radiated from her care-free personality. She had clearly grown up around a lot of men and was at ease around them. The realization made Carter finally relax. She wasn't being overfriendly with him—this was just how she was, and he didn't need to read anything into her behavior or be worried where she was concerned. He was close to Rhett's age and she was going to treat him and banter with him the same as she did her brothers. He wouldn't let his guard down because he didn't do that for anyone, but he could stop worrying.

"Park up here." Shannon pointed toward a row of diagonal parking spaces near a large grassy area. "Dr. Spira's office is over there. And his house is just beyond it, there, by the forest preserve." The little red building had a sign hanging near the front door that read All Creatures Welcome. A white two-story house sat just to the right of the red building, and an American flag suspended from the wide front porch snapped in the wind. Flowers flooded the front walkway. The house sat at the far edge of town and was surrounded by trees.

Carter parked his truck and hopped out. He rounded the vehicle to meet up with Shannon and found her frozen on the sidewalk. Her mouth was open. Her fingers shook where they were hooked onto her purse's strap. More than anything, the color in her face had fled.

Her posture made him pause. His muscles coiled, ready for an attack or whatever had made her fearful. A muscle memory from childhood.

They hadn't known each other long, but every time Carter had interacted with Shannon she had been smiling, challenging, teasing or demanding he save her pet goose. Until now, her cheeks had always had a pink tinge to them. What could make a strong woman like that freeze and shake where she stood?

Carter followed her gaze. Across the street a lean man with shaggy dirty-blond hair had his hands on his hips as he stared Shannon down. More like glared. Sickness burned through Carter's chest. The possessive way the guy was eyeing her didn't sit well with him.

It was his stepdad bearing down on his mom, fists flying, all over again.

Carter turned his back on the man and stepped into Shannon's line of vision.

She blinked as if she was waking up from a long sleep and she stumbled forward to grip Carter's arm. "Can I ask you something? To do something crazy?" Her voice trembled.

Carter stepped closer to her. Warning sirens sounded in his head. He would do whatever she needed. He would protect now when he hadn't been able to back then. "Anything."

"Pretend to be my boyfriend." She grimaced. "Just for a second. Just until—"

Carter wrapped his arms around her, tugging her to his body in a hug the same way she had hugged him yesterday. She was still shaking a little and every long-buried protective instinct clattered alive inside him. No man worth his salt caused a woman to feel terrified. He fought the urge to fist his hands, cross the street and demand answers out of the man by force. That wouldn't solve anything. And it certainly wouldn't help defuse the situation for Shannon, which was what mattered right now.

"I'm sorry." Shannon's arms were around him, too. Each of her fingertips dug into his back. Each point of contact sending the same message: *I need you.* Trusting him—a stranger—to keep her safe. "I'm so sorry I asked this of you," she whispered against his neck.

Carter's chest burned. Clearly, this was what Shannon's brothers were afraid of—why they hadn't wanted her to head into town on her own. Whoever the man across the street was, he had hurt Shannon greatly. He was a danger still.

"It's fine," Carter murmured against her hair. He hoped that from the man's vantage point it looked like they were whispering sweet nothings to each other. He eased her away, placed his hand on the small of her back and veered her toward his truck. Opening the passenger-side door, he flipped up the armrest and helped Shannon back into the cab. He climbed into the passenger seat as she scooted to the middle seat and then he slung his arm to curl protectively over her shoulders. Again, he hoped the guy could see. Hoped their body language was a clear message for him to back off and leave her alone for good, whoever he was.

The insinuation that a woman needed a man to claim her as his in order to get another man to leave her alone chafed at Carter. But sadly, he knew how men like the one across the street thought. That man would have bothered Shannon without Carter there and might have even approached them if he hadn't thought Carter was attached to her.

In the safety of the cramped truck, Shannon rocked forward and dropped her head into her hands. "I feel so stupid. I can't believe I freaked out like that." She groaned. "That wasn't how this was supposed to go down at all."

Carter placed a comforting hand on her upper back, encouraging her to keep talking if she needed to. Sometimes the presence of another person was far more important than words.

She sat up again and twisted a bit to face him better. "In my head I've run through so many scenarios of how I would react the first time I saw him again. But it was *never* that. Not panic." She slumped against the seat, which brought her right under his arm again, snug to his side. Carter debated extracting his arm but couldn't think of a nonawkward way to go about it, so he stayed where he was. He didn't mind her so close, but he wanted to make sure she was comfortable with their proximity. She seemed to be.

Carter ducked his head so he could make the eye contact she had been avoiding until then. "Are you going to tell me who that was and why he made you so scared?" He held her gaze for a heartbeat. "You don't have to if you don't want to. But if you want to talk, I'm right here."

She crossed her arms. "He's an ex. Though I'm guessing you picked up on that by now."

"He didn't treat you very well, did he?" Carter kept his voice quiet and steady.

She nodded. "I was going through a rough time when we got together. I felt, I don't know, really lonely and he was there and always wanted to be around me. At the time that felt really nice." She laughed once, but it had a bitter edge to it. "I know that sounds dumb now."

"I don't think it sounds dumb at all." He glanced in the rearview mirror. The guy was still there, his gaze trained on the truck. Carter wouldn't have minded crossing the street to confront him, but he forced himself to look away, to stay put and remain with Shannon. "I get it, believe me."

She lifted her chin but he could feel the tremors that were still working their way through her body. "Well, wanting to be together all the time turned into him wanting to control what I was doing and who I spent time with. He tried to divide me from my family—I'm ashamed to admit he succeeded for a while."

"Abusers can start out as being really convincing," Carter said.

"Abusers," she whispered. Shannon looked out the driver's-side window. Away from Carter. "When I finally started to stand up to him he got violent."

Carter rubbed the stress from his jaw.

Another woman used and broken-down and questioning herself because of the wounds inflicted by an insecure man. Carter had spent too many years watching his mother get tossed around by his stepdad. Too many horrible images were forever imprinted on his mind. Times he couldn't or didn't step up to defend her.

Times he had gotten in front of her and taken the hits came to mind, too.

Carter snaked his arm away from Shannon to fist his

hands in his lap. He ground his teeth together. "Tell me to go across the street and deal with him, and I will."

Shannon hooked her hands around Carter's closest arm, her eyes wide. "Please, don't. Cord is… I don't want him to… I don't—"

Carter forced a smile. It was shaky at best. "I won't. I wouldn't have." Well, he would have if she had asked him to. He ran his fingers over his jaw and blew out a long breath. "I'm just really angry someone treated you that way." His heart was acting like a penned ram in his chest, going berserk. He hadn't been this worked up in a long time.

Shannon let go of him and scooted further onto the driver's side of the vehicle. "So that's what I am. Now you know my story." She trailed a finger over the steering wheel. "Some weak girl who—"

"Weak?" Carter angled toward her. "Hold up there." He held out a hand. "You are not weak."

Her hands fisted the steering wheel. She kept her head pointed toward the windshield. "Did you hear anything I just said? I am."

"You're not," he said quietly.

"Everyone thinks so." She finally faced him. Her eyebrows rose with a silent question.

Don't you think so?

"You left him, didn't you?"

She bit her bottom lip. "Much later than I should have."

She had left. Didn't she understand what a big deal that was? So many never walked away.

"So you're strong and capable," he said. "Just like I thought."

She dropped her hands from the wheel. "I think a strong and capable person wouldn't have been in that situation to begin with."

"At some point in life everyone ends up in a situation they later wish they had never been in. I sure have." He shook his head. "Just remember, how someone else treats you doesn't define who you are. It only reveals who they are. What you experienced showed you this Cord guy is an abusive jerk who isn't worth your time and that you are made of strong enough stuff to stand up to him and leave," Carter said. "Don't make light of that accomplishment."

"You really don't think I'm weak?" she asked as if the answer to his question was incredibly important. It made Carter wonder if others treated Shannon in a way that made her believe that lie. Because it was a lie. She was brave and strong and capable—and if he could see that after knowing her for one day then anyone who thought otherwise had to be blind.

"The woman who demanded a stranger save her goose?" He smiled. "Let's just say I'm one hundred percent positive the word *weak* could never be applied to you." He gently added, "You left, Shannon. Many women never leave."

His mother hadn't.

A choice that had cost her life in the end.

Shannon swallowed a few times. "I never thought of it that way."

They were getting in too deep, touching on too many

of his past wounds that he had long ago bandaged up and promised he wouldn't poke anymore. If he talked any longer she would pick up on the fact that he was speaking from experience, if she hadn't already.

She was safe. This Cord guy wasn't approaching her. They could move on.

"Ready to go get your goose?" He jutted his head in the direction of the little red building. Then he opened the passenger door and held out his hand to help her across the seat and out the door. He dropped it just as quickly. Cord was no longer across the street.

They didn't need to act any longer.

Wing Crosby honked from his place in the pet carrier tucked between Shannon and Carter in the truck. Shannon peeked into the carrier and couldn't help the smile on her face.

They had ended up visiting with Dr. Spira for more than an hour at his clinic and then Carter had assisted the doctor when someone rushed in with a bundle of abandoned kittens who were clearly starving. After all of that, they had ended up being in town for three hours.

Carter narrowed his eyes as if the incessant honking was giving him a headache. "He's going to honk like that the whole way home, isn't he?"

"It's not honking," Shannon said. "He's crooning for you, Carter. You should be honored."

"Crooning. Right." Carter hooked his hand over the top of the steering wheel but Shannon caught the glint of humor clear in his eye. When Rhett had first told her he had hired someone to fill the vacant head wrangler position, she had feared he would find someone just like himself. She loved her eldest brother, but he was so serious and withdrawn most of the time. Rhett was happier alone in his office than among a crowd. She was glad Carter hadn't ended up being what she expected. With Wade and Rhett always busy with their new families, it was nice to have someone around in her age group to visit with who actually seemed to enjoy talking and joking.

It didn't hurt that he smelled like leather and spice and late-night walks.

Or that he had called her capable and strong and looked at her as if he was proud of her.

How someone else treats you doesn't define who you are. It only reveals who they are.

Well, his actions had revealed Carter to be a kind and compassionate man who cared about animals and was willing to lend a hand, or a hug when needed. And the intensity in his eyes when they had spoken in the truck had stolen her breath. She didn't doubt for a second that he would have risen to her defense if he had needed to.

Beyond her family, she rarely shared with anyone what had happened to her. But she felt as if she could trust Carter.

Then again, hadn't she recently decided to stop trusting her feelings?

She poked a finger through the carrier and Wing immediately butted his head against her. "Please tell me you're a Bing Crosby fan. Because I don't know if we can be friends if you're not."

Carter made a noncommittal sound.

"Come on," Shannon urged. "*White Christmas* is a holiday staple. Tell me you've at least seen that one."

"I mean, I watch it if I happen to catch it on TV, if that's what you're asking."

"Oh, no way. That's not good enough. Watching *White Christmas* is an event. There has to be cookie making and popcorn and comfy blankets."

Carter made a show of peering out the windows. "You know it's not Christmas, right? You're three months late."

She crossed her arms. "Have you seen *The Bells of St. Mary's*?"

He shook his head.

"What about *My Favorite Brunette*?"

He gave a little shrug. "What can I say? I've always liked blondes."

When he peeked her way, Shannon rolled her eyes in a teasing way.

She made a mental note to invite Carter to the next old-movie marathon she planned. For the last few years, about once a month she had invited staff members to movie parties. Sometimes she threw themed parties and sometimes it was more of a spur-of-the-moment marathon. Though lately she had been doing more watching on her own than she would like. Before they were both married to her brothers, Macy and Cassidy used to join Shannon for movies. But Shannon understood they needed time with their new husbands now.

She needed to start making new traditions. Her life shouldn't be on hold just because her best friends had gotten married. Shannon made a promise to herself to start being more social again.

"Fear not, I'll help you get caught up on Bing Crosby movies. I could plan a staff party around it." Wing Crosby honked again. "Something spring themed to celebrate coming on one year since the tornado. We could host it at the barn—use a tarp to project the movie on the side of the building. I've seen that online."

"Sure." Carter chuckled. "We'll hang those twinkle lights in the barn and maybe wrap some flower garlands around Memphis for kicks."

Shannon sat up straighter. "That's not a half-bad idea."

"I was kidding."

"I'm not."

"Memphis won't like garland wrapped around him. I promise. He'd probably eat it."

She remembered the pageant sign that hung in the middle of Stillwater and an idea clicked into place. "Carter, I'm serious. You just gave me the best idea." One that would give her something to focus on, a way to benefit the ranch. She could finally raise money for the indoor riding center she had wanted to build and, more than anything, do something that could be her project. She would have to run the idea past Rhett, of course, but she would make a point of not letting any of her siblings or their spouses help out. This would be her contribution to the ranch. Something her brothers could come to and see how successful she could be if they would just trust her.

By the time they got back to Red Dog Ranch, Shannon was so excited she could have hugged Carter. Again.

But twice in two days of knowing each other was probably already far more than Carter had wanted. She definitely hadn't minded, though. Carter had been really great when they were in town and he had encouraged her about the Cord situation in a way no one else ever had. Something about the new head wrangler put her at ease.

She spotted Rhett, Macy, Wade, Cassidy and their daughter, Piper, gathered near the front enclosure that housed the ranch's miniature pony and overly affectionate donkey.

Carter tossed the truck into Park and picked up Wing Crosby's carrier. Shannon exited the truck and rushed around the vehicle to meet up with him. He started to hand the carrier over to her when Rhett called to them.

"Come on over here. I want to introduce Carter to everyone."

Carter shot out a long breath before heading in their direction. It was funny to see that he was nervous around her family. They were just her siblings and all of them were nice.

Wade greeted them with a huge, lopsided grin. "Ah, good. I see you brought Thanksgiving Dinner home." He pulled Shannon into a side hug.

She elbowed her twin brother in the ribs. "Stop calling him that."

Piper, Wade's spunky five-year-old daughter, skipped up to her dad's side and took his hand. "Are we really going to eat Wing?" Her brow scrunched. "I really don't want to."

Shannon hugged the pet carrier to her body. "Not ever."

"No, sweetheart. Daddy just thinks he's funny." Cassidy, Wade's wife, hooked her arm through Wade's free one. They made the picture of the ideal family—attractive, young and so in love with each other—no one would suspect how much they had gone through in order to be together. Only nine months ago, Cassidy had believed Wade to be dead, and then after a few bumps, they had faced his cancer diagnosis and treatment together.

Once Wade had introduced his family to Carter, they headed out.

"I've been told we're headed to the Riverwalk for some ice cream." Wade scooped up Piper as they walked away.

Piper sent Shannon a wink over his shoulder. "It was my idea. I told him."

Cassidy laughed and joined her husband and daughter.

Rhett had an arm around Macy when he introduced her to Carter. Macy was seven months pregnant, but she hadn't let that slow her down around the ranch until lately. Shannon had enjoyed watching her "man's man" brother turn into a family guy who fawned over his wife and their expected child. At heart, her big brother was a huge softy. Nearby, Kodiak, Rhett's ever-faithful shadow of a dog, and Cloudstorm, Piper's gray-and-white cat, lounged in the grass. The two pets had finally come to some sort of an understanding.

That, or Kodiak had finally gotten it through her head that Cloudstorm was the boss around these parts.

After Rhett finished introducing Carter to Macy, he turned to Shannon. "How did lessons go?"

"Good. We worked on emergency dismounts today."

"No one got hurt, did they?" he asked.

She took a breath before answering, calming her frustration. He would have asked the question to anyone, wouldn't he? She hoped so.

"I know the ranch's protocol. I would have called you if someone got hurt." She set Wing's carrier down and opened the door, letting him waddle out. He honked and ducked through the opening, shaking his tail feathers in an indignant way. He probably would have appreciated being let out of the carrier the second they got back.

Ever a birding dog, Kodiak's ears perked up as her amber eyes followed Wing's movements. But Shannon knew Rhett's dog was incredibly well trained and wouldn't lurch at her pet goose without Rhett's blessing. Rhett had been a professional dog trainer before he had inherited Red Dog Ranch. Cloudstorm eyed Wing, but Wing had chased after Cloudstorm on occasion, so Shannon knew he could hold his own if the cat got any dumb ideas.

Shannon patted Wing Crosby's head one last time and then faced Rhett again. "There's actually something I wanted to run past you. An event I want to plan."

Rhett and Macy stepped a little closer.

"I'd love to hear about it," Macy said. She reached up

to entwine her fingers with the hand of the arm Rhett had draped over her shoulders.

Shannon motioned for Carter to join them. He lifted his eyebrows but stepped into their little family huddle. "It was actually Carter's idea."

Carter's head jerked back. "Wait. What was my idea?" His gaze sought hers.

Shannon plowed ahead. "What if we hosted a fun spring horse show as a fund-raiser?" She held up a hand when Rhett opened his mouth. "Hear me out. People would have to pay an entrance fee and we could have a horse-and-rider costume contest and maybe run some other events like they do at any normal horse show. We can advertise it as something to celebrate the one-year mark from the tornado—show how we have rebuilt and moved forward." She was thinking and speaking on the fly, so she tossed out ideas as they came. "If we have it a week or two before Easter we can invite vendors to set up shops at the event. There would be a small vendor fee." She added quickly, "And all the money raised can go into a fund to finally build the riding arena."

Macy's smile widened. "I think that sounds like a great idea. We had to scale back the egg hunt this year, so I know the community would appreciate an event to replace it." Macy had always helped to plan the annual egg hunt, which had spawned into a grand affair that had cost a lot of money to run. Funds that were better spent helping foster children in more tangible ways. The ranch was still going to host a small egg hunt for local foster children who already utilized its other programs, but this year's event wouldn't be open to the public like it had been in the past.

Rhett rubbed his chin. "I don't know. You'd have three or four weeks tops to plan, organize and promote the event. Gathering vendors and participants in that time... I'm not sure that's doable."

Macy swatted her husband's chest. "This man of mine is forgetting that he and I threw together the egg hunt last year in even less time."

Rhett captured his wife's hand and pressed a kiss to her palm before tucking her close against him again. "My lovely wife is leaving out the fact that the egg hunt had been a longstanding annual tradition we already had all the information on file for. We weren't building something brand-new on a short deadline."

"Just let her try," Macy gently urged.

Rhett sighed. "We'll do everything we can to help you."

Shannon hesitated. As much as she loved her siblings and their wives, if she let them get involved they would take over without even meaning to. And she didn't want that. The whole point was to show them what she could do without them. To prove she could do something that was valuable to the ranch.

To make them proud, for once.

"Well, the thing is I'm going to plan this alone."

Macy's mouth went slack. "That's just not possible. You need at least another hand. Let me—"

"Not alone, alone," Shannon quickly added. She hooked her arm with Carter's. "Carter's going to plan the event with me. It was his idea, after all."

Carter's mouth opened, closed, opened again. "It really wasn't my idea."

"It was. He joked about decorating the horses and that's where the idea started."

Rhett looked at the new head wrangler. "Are you willing to help my sister with this? It will be a lot of extra work."

Carter looked to Shannon and she tried to use her eyes to plead with him. He took off his hat and ran his hand over his hair. "Do you want me to, sir?"

"Well, she's definitely not doing it on her own," Rhett said.

Shannon swallowed the hot wave of emotions Rhett's heavy-handed words caused. She knew he loved her. Knew he never meant to hurt her. But sometimes his matter-of-fact way of stating things did just that. She didn't want to plan the event on her own, either, but Rhett could have handled the conversation better.

Carter dipped his head once, acknowledging what Rhett had said. "Then it looks like I'm going to help plan a spring horse show."

Shannon could have hugged him.

She didn't.

But she definitely could have.

Chapter Four

Carter was mucking out his fifth stall the next morning when the barn door creaked. He glanced up, expecting it to be another one of the ranch hands stopping in to pick up their mount for the day.

Wing Crosby honked softly from his perch on top of a hay bale in the hallway. The goose had been sitting outside his bunkhouse when he left in the morning and had waddled behind him the whole way to the barn. Wing had been dozing on and off for the past hour while Carter worked, though if Carter disappeared outside for too long the little gander came looking for him.

Carter had already saddled and passed out three horses that morning, but this time it wasn't a ranch hand walking toward him. Instead, Shannon sauntered in with a large thermos in one hand and brown bag in the other.

He leaned on the pitchfork and watched her approach. She had jeans, boots and a pink flannel button-up on.

With her blond curls and the ever-present quirk of a smile, she was a beautiful woman.

What was she doing there?

After the run-in with her ex-boyfriend, it had been difficult to shake thoughts of Shannon from his mind last night. How long had she dated Cord? Had she loved him? Carter kept thinking about how she had felt in his arms when they had hugged and how nice it had been to have someone need him—believe him capable of protecting them, for once.

But his thoughts had cleared by morning. Thinking about Shannon in any capacity beyond that of his boss's sister was dangerous. After their interactions yesterday, he had hoped to put some space between them for a few days. He knew he couldn't get attached. They could never be friends.

If she knew him she wouldn't have clung to him.

Probably wouldn't even want him at the ranch.

Shannon cocked her head as she made her way down the walkway between stables. "We missed you at breakfast." She stopped a few feet away from him. A warm, sweet smell wafted from the bag she carried, making his stomach tighten. While Rhett had informed Carter meals were often served in the mess hall during the week, he had failed to tell him what times those meals took place. Carter hadn't wanted to wander in too early or too late and risk looking foolish.

Over the weekend he had eaten through his meager stash of granola bars and canned soup, but this morning he had just gone without.

Later, he would head into town and pick up some

groceries. It made sense to have a few odds and ends at his house. He shouldn't be solely dependent on the Jarretts to feed him, even if that was part of his job perks. Besides, in the thirteen years he had lived on his own he had learned enough about cooking to scrape together respectable meals when he needed to.

Her eyes narrowed. "Rhett forgot to tell you when to be there, didn't he?"

Carter shifted his weight off the pitchfork. "I've gone without food before. It hasn't killed me yet."

"Only because you haven't tasted Cassidy's homemade buttermilk waffles. If you had, then you would know what a crime it was to miss out on these treasures." She lofted the brown bag. "Thankfully, since I was looking out for you, you won't have to face that sort of breakfast doom."

"Breakfast doom?" Despite warning himself to stay aloof, he fought a grin. Quickly he was discovering it was difficult to act detached when Shannon was around. She possessed the dangerous ability to put him at ease. He thawed around her, more than he cared to admit. "You have a funny way of saying things."

"Grow up with three older brothers and you'd talk like this, too." She shook the bag. "Wash up and then follow me." She jerked her chin and headed toward the office. Her tone invited no argument.

Carter stowed the pitchfork and headed to the washroom to scrub his hands and forearms. He wasn't sure why Shannon had stopped by, but he couldn't exactly tell her to leave so he could go back to work. Not that he minded the interruption, but he did have twenty-eight horses to deworm and had wanted to get that done before lunch. He knew the old practice of deworming horses every six months was considered out-of-date, but he had been over all the horses' records last night and hadn't found any indication they had been dewormed in the past two years. He planned to work on half of the herd today and the other tomorrow. He would start with the younger horses.

As he headed into the office, his stomach grumbled.

Shannon had gathered all the papers from the desk into a neat pile and had laid out a plate and silverware in their place. She pulled various containers from the brown bag and went to work filling the plate.

Carter paused in the doorway. "What's going on here?"

"Remember I said I saved you from breakfast doom?" She arranged a waffle, bacon and slices of cantaloupe on the plate. "Don't pretend you're not hungry. I heard your stomach grumble."

Carter laid a self-conscious hand on his abdomen. "You heard that, huh?"

"Oh, I'm pretty sure they heard in Louisiana." She opened the thermos and poured a dark pink liquid into a glass jar. "Cassidy's blueberry lemonade. It's beyond words, trust me." She thrust the glass into his hand.

Carter took a tentative sip and then went back for a large gulp of the drink. It was a refreshing mix of tang and sweetness. He finally set the cup down. "Is that honey?"

Shannon nodded. "Cassidy would be impressed you were able to pick that out with all the flavors."

Carter rubbed at the back of his neck. While he was touched that Shannon had thought about him again, the attention made him uncomfortable. In his experience, people weren't kind just to be kind—there was always a string attached or a catch involved. He had learned the hard way that it was better to be direct and up-front from the get-go, even if the approach rarely won him friends.

After all, he wasn't here to make friends.

Shannon motioned for him to take a seat.

Carter folded his arms over his chest. "I enjoy your company, so don't take this the wrong way." He gestured toward the food. "But what is all this?"

Shannon's mouth opened then closed. She dropped into the chair on the other side of the desk. "It's food, Carter. You know, the stuff we need for our bodies to have energy to live and move and work. Scientific types call it calories." She laid her hand against her breastbone. "I call it delicious."

He had to give it to her: she wasn't ruffled by his straightforward manner at all. Most people were. "I track with that part fine, but not the part about you going out of your way to bring it to me." He knew his manner still had the possibility of pushing her away, but maybe it would be better if she did turn and run. She would eventually.

Everyone did.

She shook her head. "You're weird. You know that? Most guys would be thrilled if a girl brought them food. Most guys would dig right in."

Carter stayed rooted to his spot. "I'm not most guys."

"Noted." Shannon leaned back in the chair. "For what it's worth, I did not *go out of my way*—" she mimicked his voice with impressive accuracy "—to bring you anything." She tugged a pad of paper from the brown bag. "I had to stop here to meet with you so we could start planning the horse show. I came from the dining hall and Cassidy packed that food, not me. She went on some tangent about you being only the second person to ever avoid her meals. So there, your mystery is solved."

"Sorry," Carter mumbled. He scrubbed the back of his neck, feeling a bit like a chided dog. Shannon hadn't been put off by his blunt approach; instead she had flipped the conversation on its head and put him in his place. He had to respect a person who could do that with a smile and a laugh in their voice.

He relaxed his stance and headed to the empty chair. After all, he *was* hungry and the food was getting cold. It had been thoughtful of Cassidy and Shannon to help out a new staff member. Given his curt response, Carter felt as if he owed Shannon more of an explanation. "Where I come from, people don't just do nice things for others."

She tucked her pencil behind her ear. "Did you ever stop to consider maybe *that's* weird, not me?"

Carter shook his head and dropped down into the seat. "You're not weird."

She cocked her head. "You're sure acting like I am."

"I find you intriguing." Far more dangerous than weird would have been.

Her eyes widened.

Why had he said that? He needed to steer the conversation back toward neutral ground. He focused on cutting the waffle. "You were serious about the horse show?"

She had ambushed him yesterday in front of Rhett and he hadn't been about to turn his boss down. But later on, Carter had hoped that Shannon would abandon that idea as too much work and he would be off the hook.

Then again, when had his life ever taken the easiest route?

She dropped the notepad and her cell phone onto his desk, jabbing her pencil against the paper. "Oh, we're doing this and we're going to make it amazing. Nothing short of that, okay? I want people to say this was the best event they have ever attended at Red Dog Ranch. Got it?"

Apparently, Shannon wasn't the give-up type.

Carter winked at her. "No pressure."

"Wrong." She pointed the pencil at him. "We like pressure—we're going to embrace every moment of it. Know why? Because pressure turns coal into diamonds."

Carter set his fork down. He wanted to joke, but she was looking at him like he was her lifeline. With such a mixture of hope and expectation, as if she considered him someone she could fully depend on.

No one had ever looked at him like that before.

His throat went momentarily dry and his voice was raw when he said, "This is really important to you."

Shannon pursed her lips and set down her pencil as she glanced toward the open office door, clearly gauging if anyone was around to overhear them. She leaned forward in her chair, her voice low. "Between you and me, this might be the most important thing I've ever done. Maybe my reasons don't make sense, but it has to do with what you saw yesterday."

"You're planning the horse show for your old boyfriend?" No longer hungry, Carter pushed the plate of half-eaten food to the side. Tightness pulled across his chest. He prayed she wasn't still hung up on Cord. So many women lost themselves to men who didn't deserve such devotion and many people ended up returning to abusive relationships.

"I need to think of a better way to explain everything." Shannon closed her eyes and pressed her fingertips to her forehead as if she was thinking really hard. In that moment, everything about her was adorable. He would have been content to sit with her all day.

Carter immediately shoved the thought away.

She dropped her hands to her knees. "Okay, so I have three older brothers. Do you know what it's like being a girl with three older brothers?"

Leaning back in his chair, Carter crossed his arms. "Can't say that I do."

Shannon sighed. "Don't get me wrong. They are great—really great—and they love me so much, but they can be super overprotective. Though I think that's every big brother."

His gut churned as he thought about Amy. What would his sister say about him if she were in Shannon's shoes? Amy definitely wouldn't call him protective. Perhaps she blamed him for everything like his mother had.

He had failed her miserably.

Failed them both.

Shannon's voice broke through his thoughts. "In high school no guy was brave enough to even ask me to a dance, let alone ask me out. My brothers made sure of that. And so many girls ended up only being friends with me because they had a crush on one of my brothers."

Carter tried to track with her, though he wasn't sure what dating in high school had to do with planning the horse show. "Sorry, that sounds horrible."

She shrugged. "My brothers were so determined to protect me that they ended up making it so I could never make my own mistakes or live my own life without one of them swooping in to help—even if I didn't want help." She smoothed her thumb back and forth over a rip in the armrest. "I know they've always wanted the best for me, but sometimes the best might have been letting me fail."

She let out a long breath. "Then I did fail—with what happened with Cord—and ever since then my brothers have gone back to being those guys from high school who feel like they have to flatten every bump in my road to take care of me and put me in Bubble Wrap so I can't get hurt. And on the one hand, I get it. I have a hard time trusting myself these days so I have to imagine they are nervous for me, too. But on the other hand, how will I learn to trust myself if I never learn by trial and error?"

Carter wanted to remind her that what happened with her ex wasn't failure. Someone using and abusing her was not a failure on her part—it only showed the man to be a failure as a person. But he knew she was trying to make a point and he didn't want to sidetrack her.

She tucked her hair behind her ears and then picked the pencil back up. "I know it's because my brothers love me. I get that. But it's all a little suffocating sometimes." She jiggled the pencil in a nervous motion. "All that to say, I want to run something—do something here at the ranch—that is successful without their help."

I want to matter.

I want what I do to count for something.

Her unspoken words were clear and they called to all the wounded parts of Carter's heart.

Everything finally clicked into place. He nodded. "You want to prove they can trust you."

She scooted forward in her chair with the pencil poised above the paper. "Which will never happen unless we start planning, so I'm going to need your best ideas here, cowboy." She straightened her shoulders, clearly done with the other line of conversation. "And I'm going to need them now." Shannon met his gaze and her smile was so warm and welcoming it made him feel as if he belonged. Unsettling, because Carter hadn't belonged anywhere since he was a teenager, and even then he hadn't been wanted at his stepfather's home.

Not that it mattered. Carter didn't *want* to belong anywhere or to anyone. Years ago, it had been hard enough to give his life to God. To choose to belong to God. But trusting any part of himself to a person? No chance.

Longing for connection would only end in a pain he never wanted to experience again.

Still, he couldn't deny there was a piece of home in Shannon's smile. A piece of home Carter had never known before. He could very well have lost himself in the moment and forgotten that he wasn't interested in a relationship.

He could have forgotten if she hadn't been the boss's sister.

But she was.

They had spent the past forty-five minutes brainstorming for the horse show. After their first five minutes, Wing Crosby had waddled into the office and nestled down between Carter's desk and a file cabinet. He was sound asleep now, his head tucked on top of his back.

Shannon scribbled another note into the margin of her pad of paper. "I really think a costume contest is a must."

When one of Carter's eyebrows went up, she held out a hand to stop whatever he was about to say. "Stick with me, here. A costume contest sets us apart from all the other shows in this area—especially a costume contest in spring. It gives the event a bigger draw. People who might not have come out to see barrel racing will bring their kids to see horses and riders dressed up in silly outfits."

Carter leaned forward. He seemed so at-home in the tiny office amongst the smells of straw and dust and the mixed scents of horse sweat and leather. Despite having only just arrived, the man belonged in this barn in a way none of her brothers ever had.

"You've got a point," he said. "We may want to come up with some guidelines, though. Maybe a theme would help."

Shannon jotted the word *theme* on the paper and put a huge question mark next to it. "Let's table that until tomorrow. I want to think over the pros and cons of limiting what people are allowed to do before making a decision." Of course, they would have rules to keep everything wholesome and to make sure safety was a top priority, but if they limited the costumes to something like princess-themed costumes, for example, then they would also be restricting their entries. More people signing up meant more entry fees.

Easton stuck his head into the office. "I'm here. What do you want me to do today?"

Wing Crosby made an indignant snuffling sound as his head swung up. He eyed Easton, clearly annoyed that the young man had interrupted his nap.

Carter scrunched his brow for a moment. "Finish mucking the stalls, but before you turn the ones in here out, remember what we talked about yesterday."

Easton nodded. "Horsemanship is in the details. Paying attention to the little things is what separates a great cowboy from a mediocre one because a good horseman checks over his animals and notices every change in behavior and temperament every single day."

"Exactly." Carter grinned, pride washing over his features. "Good memory."

Easton rolled his eyes. "You only said it like fifty-seven times."

Wearing the coat Carter had lent him the other day, the teenager headed back into the barn. Shannon couldn't help but notice the warm admiration in Carter's eyes as he watched Easton leave. It was evident that he cared about the boy and wanted to help him. Easton had worked with Wade the first few weeks he had volunteered at Red Dog Ranch but had back-talked her twin so much the Jarretts had considered telling Easton he had to take a break from the program. At that point Rhett had switched Easton to helping Shannon with the horses and he had been doing that for the past few weeks. Shannon had put up with the boy's attitude because she hadn't wanted her brothers to ask him to leave, but Carter seemed to have a way of dealing with the young man's sarcastic moods while still getting him to work respectfully.

With Easton gone, she focused on the reason she had sought Carter out today. Before she entered the barn, Shannon had feared that perhaps she had been too rash in offering to plan an event on such a short deadline. What if they couldn't pull it off? What if the horse show crashed and burned and Shannon failed hugely in a public way?

No one cares about what you have to say.

You're nothing without me.

Everyone would be disappointed if they knew the real you.

Most days it took a lot of effort to turn Cord's voice off in her head and often she wasn't completely successful. But meeting with Carter had actually helped chase Cord's words away. He had enthusiastically offered suggestions and been an equal partner in the conversation so far. As they planned and tossed out ideas, her anxiety had ebbed. He hadn't laughed at or belittled a single suggestion she had made.

But she couldn't stay here with him all day. No matter

how much she wanted to. After all, Carter had work to get done other than the horse show. She needed to wrap things up. "We still have to think about vendors if we want to have booths outside the show area. I still think that's a good idea, what about you?"

He drummed his fingers on the desk. "Craft booths, food tents and local vendors—I don't see why not."

"Any other ideas?" Even though her paper was almost out of room, she held her pencil ready.

"I once helped at a Christmas horse show and we had some of the teams run through a course while the rider held a full cup of eggnog. Whoever spilled the least won," Carter said. "We could replace the eggnog with something else."

"With lemonade," Shannon offered as she added Carter's idea to the others. "That could be a lot of fun." Another idea hit her. "If I'm remembering correctly, I think the ranch has a connection to a professional barrel racer. She was a camper here at one point. How cool would it be if she showed up?"

Carter nodded. "That could be a good draw."

"I don't remember her name but maybe Rhett or Wade will." She would ask them about it tonight. Shannon scooped the notepad up and hugged it to her chest. "This may actually work, Carter. I can't thank you enough for helping me even though I know Rhett didn't give you much of a choice." She dropped the notes into her bag and stood. "I'm going to head back to my place to start working on a list of people and places we need to contact and what materials we need to make this happen. We'll start pounding the pavement tomorrow."

He smoothed his hand over the desktop. "You mentioned your brothers."

Shannon paused on her way to the door. "I did." She looked back at him, but Carter was studying his hands. After a long pause, he met her gaze.

"Have you told them?" His voice was so soft.

She tilted her head, regarding him. "Um, you were there yesterday when I did."

"Not about the horse show, I mean about how you feel about them being overprotective." Carter got out of his chair and moved to the front of the desk. He leaned against it and crossed his arms. "All that stuff you told me earlier—have you ever said those things to them?"

Shannon's stomach tightened as she took a step closer to him. She kept her voice low so Easton wouldn't be able to overhear. "It would hurt their feelings."

"But aren't *they* hurting yours right now?"

"That's not fair." She swallowed once, twice. She didn't want Carter to get the wrong impression of the Jarrett men. "My brothers are good people—some of the best people I've ever met—and they would never intentionally hurt anyone. Least of all me."

His eyebrows rose. "Which brings me back to…you should say something. How can they change their behavior if they're unaware of how you feel?"

She knew what Carter was saying made sense, but after hearing Cord tell her that what she had to say didn't matter or she was making too big of a deal out of something or she didn't understand and he knew better, speaking up about her feelings had become a scary adventure. Even to people she loved…especially to people she loved. She had thought she loved Cord and had assumed he loved her and had been acting in a loving manner.

She had been so wrong.

What if she talked to her brothers and they shrugged her off or said they knew better? She would like to believe they wouldn't—her brothers weren't like that—but still, the fear of it happening lingered, and after what she had been through, she couldn't shake it.

Shannon loved Rhett, Wade and Boone too much to risk having tension with any of them. She knew they loved her and were acting how they were because they were worried about her. If the horse show was successful they would start to back off. They would see she was okay and she was getting better. She didn't need to talk to them about it, because her plan would work.

Carter dropped his arms from his chest, his hands gripping the edge of the desk instead as if he was rooting himself there. "Maybe I shouldn't say anything." His voice was warm and soft. "But part of overcoming an abuser is realizing that even after you leave, they want you to feel lost and alone. They want you to feel as if you aren't allowed to speak up for yourself ever again. That's how they maintain power."

A hot wave of tears gathered in Shannon's eyes. She swallowed hard. Every word he spoke mirrored a deep, dark fear that grew in her heart's soil. No matter how many times over the past nine months she had tried to pull out the weeds Cord had planted, they kept coming back. They continued to strangle her every attempt at growth.

"How do you know so much about this?" she whispered.

He spoke on the subject as if he was a trained counselor or someone who had lived through it. A tingle of unease washed over Shannon's shoulders. Had Carter been in an abusive relationship…or had he been the abuser? Everything about him screamed that only the first option was possible. Besides, someone capable of abuse wouldn't lay out a game plan used by abusers like Carter just had, would they?

Her mind was making strange leaps, but she had misjudged a man before and doing so had almost cost her everything.

Shannon took a step backward.

Carter didn't seem to notice. "The *how* doesn't matter. What matters is that you never needed Cord or anyone to be complete. And when you left him, you took the power over your life back into your hands, so now the question is…what are you going to do with that power?"

She hugged her stomach. "I don't know."

"Be heard, Shannon. God gave you a voice so you could use it."

Shannon made her excuses and left, only to hurry back to her house and shed the tears she'd been holding in for weeks. Maybe months. She had thought leaving Cord would be the hardest part, but it had only been the beginning. Sometimes it felt as if unwinding his lies and healing were going to take the rest of her life.

And maybe Cord *had* been right about one thing. Maybe she was damaged goods that no one else would ever be able to love.

Chapter Five

Shannon cut another slice of raspberry-cream pie and dished it onto a second plate. Ever since Rhett and Macy had gotten married, dispersing the other siblings from the large family ranch house, the family had made a point of gathering at Rhett and Macy's once a week to spend time together. Cassidy always brought dessert.

Shannon glanced across the room. The large kitchen flowed into an eating area and a two-story-tall living room. An entire wall of the living room was made of windows. Carter's suggestion to speak to her brothers about their overprotectiveness went through her mind. While Shannon could admit that Carter's advice had merit, now wasn't the time to speak with them. Not when everyone was together and so happy.

In her experience, most guys wouldn't have cared about helping her have healthy relationships with her family. And even if they cared, they wouldn't have felt comfortable calling her out for not being forthright with her brothers. Shannon found she liked Carter's straightforward way. There was no manipulation or falseness in how he handled things and he didn't strike her as one to sugarcoat things. After being lied to and led on by Cord, it was refreshing to spend time with someone who was exactly what they seemed to be. Someone who had no interest in playing mind games.

Tiny Piper was sprawled on the floor, where she, Wade and Rhett were engaged in an involved game of dinosaur-themed Go Fish. Kodiak lay close to Rhett's side. Cassidy was seated in the chair beside Shannon's mom, her hands cupping one of the elderly woman's while they spoke in soft tones, heads bent together. Their mother's Alzheimer's had steadily worsened in the year since their father had passed away. Tonight she seemed more worn down than usual. Rhett had told Shannon their mother hadn't been sleeping well for a long time and his concerns about her care were growing.

Earlier, they had used a tablet to video-chat with Boone, his wife, June, and their daughter, Hailey. Boone and his family were living in Maine while Boone finished his seminary degree but the family was hopeful that they would be able to settle back in Texas eventually. Shannon really missed Boone. While she was indisputably closest to her twin, she had a good relationship with each of her brothers.

Macy eased herself onto a seat at the kitchen table, her hand resting on top of her abdomen. With a plate of pie in each hand, Shannon joined her pregnant sister-in-law. She scooted a plate in Macy's direction. Kodiak plodded up to Macy's side and laid her head in her lap. The dog had always been attached to Rhett, but since about the midway point in Macy's pregnancy Kodiak had started staying closer to her than to Rhett.

"Do you remember the name of the professional barrel racer who used to be a camper here?" Shannon asked. "I wanted to get in contact with her and see if she would be willing to attend our horse show."

"You're talking about Violet Byrd." Macy tugged her phone from her pocket. "I have her number if you want it. Or I can call her for you."

"I'll call her." Shannon felt her pockets but couldn't locate her phone. The last time she remembered having it, she had been at the barn with Carter.

Macy's eyebrow rose. "Lose something?"

Shannon shook her head. "I just left my phone somewhere."

"Before you got here we were all talking, and Rhett said money was missing from his wallet the other day and Wade had a pair of expensive sunglasses go missing," Macy said. "We were trying to figure out if it was coincidence or something we should be concerned about."

"Wade has a habit of misplacing things. I'm sure his sunglasses will turn up." Shannon found a receipt on the table and flipped it over, copying down Violet's phone number.

Macy lifted her fork, cutting into the pie. She sighed. "I know Cassidy loves her fruit desserts but sometimes I just want some chocolate. Especially now." She glanced down at her baby bump. Being a petite person, Macy was beginning to look uncomfortably pregnant at seven months.

Shannon swallowed a small bite of the pie. It was cool and tangy, with just the right amount of sweetness. Chocolate was more to Shannon's liking, too, but anything Cassidy made was good. "How have you been feeling?"

Macy rubbed her stomach as a soft smile played across her face. "Some days I can't wait to meet him, and other days I'm a little afraid of all the changes and responsibilities his arrival will bring."

Shannon laid her hand on Macy's arm. "You and Rhett are going to be amazing parents. Just look at him." Shannon jutted her chin in her eldest brother's direction. Piper had launched herself at Rhett and had her arms looped around his neck. Rhett spun her around and a tickle war began. Piper shrieked and called for her dad to join her side of the battle.

Wade laughed. "Sorry, sweetheart, but I'm afraid Rhett could pin us both at once, even if I tried." He crossed to where his wife was sitting and looped an arm around her shoulders as he pressed a kiss to the top of her head.

"No way, I'm going to win." Piper's brow set into a line of determination seconds before she scrambled around to Rhett's back. With dramatic flair, Rhett fell forward and pretended that Piper was holding him to the ground. Piper whooped in triumph and looked to her parents.

Macy hid a grin behind her hand. "He's a natural, isn't he? It's so sweet."

Once they finished their dessert, Macy ended up joining Rhett to cuddle together in a large overstuffed chair as they started a superhero movie. Cassidy had her head on Wade's shoulder and Piper was draped over both of their laps on the couch. Their mother had dozed off in her reclining chair.

Thickness coated Shannon's throat as she gazed at all of them. As much as she tried to accept the fact that perhaps she wasn't meant to find love, her heart still longed for it. Looking down, she studied the grains in the kitchen table. She couldn't sit here with her family, not tonight. Not when being around them and seeing their happiness made her physically ache.

Quietly, Shannon rose from the table and slipped on her shoes. She crossed to the living room and set a hand on Wade's shoulder. "I'm heading out. Love you, guys."

He grinned up at her. "You still don't like action movies, do you?"

Old-fashioned romance movies were more her style but that realization made her sad. Words clogging in her throat, she waved at everyone and headed outside. Shannon hugged her middle on her way down the front steps. Darkness had gathered over the ranch while she had been inside the old family home. She squinted past the field to the row of staff houses, where she lived. Light from the horse barn drew her attention. Had Carter forgotten to turn it off?

Not ready to be alone at her house, Shannon veered toward the barn.

"I guess that medicine helped you a bit, huh?" Carter leaned over the stall door so he could trail his fingertips along Tater Tot's tan shoulder. The buckskin had started to worry him a few hours ago, but for now the horse was calm. Still, when it came to horses, colic could go from nothing to a death sentence quickly, and Carter wasn't about to take any chances. "Too bad for you, though." He scratched Tater Tot's forehead. "You're stuck with me all night."

Wing Crosby rose and trailed after Carter as he made his way to the office and started the coffee maker. He'd unearthed the machine when he had cleaned and reorganized the space earlier that day. Then Carter headed to where hay bales were stacked like a giant pyramid against the far wall of the barn. When he dropped down onto one, the goose shook his tail feathers before hopping up beside Carter on the bale. Pressing close to Carter's thigh, Wing made himself comfortable.

"You're like a parasite. You know that?" Carter petted the goose's white feathers. The bird had followed on his heels most of the day. "I can't seem to shake you."

Wing gave a tired little honk and nestled his head onto his back. His blue eyes shuttered to a close as he tucked his beak under one of his wings. Within minutes the gander started letting out small whistling snores.

Carter leaned heavily against the bales behind him. Earlier in the evening, he had watched Shannon cross the field to the big house to spend time with her family. The sight had driven him to his office to pray. Why did God place some people into amazing families like the Jarretts while Carter had been saddled with a dad who had left and a mom who had looked the other way when her children were hurting?

Carter sighed and fished his phone from his back

pocket. He went into his contacts and stared at the screen—at his sister's name. Did she even still use the same number? They hadn't spoken in two years and he doubted she wanted to hear from him now. If she had blocked his number, he wouldn't blame her. The last time they had talked she had begged him to attend their mom's funeral and he had refused. He wouldn't disturb Amy's peace now by imposing on her with a call.

But as much as he claimed to be a man who needed no one, Carter longed for connections. How different his life would have been if he had grown up with a tight-knit group of siblings, with a family who had weekly hangout nights as the Jarretts did. His chest hurt with the want of someone to share a tie with.

Like it or not, his dad was all he had.

Without giving it much thought, he pressed the green call button. It was earlier in the evening on the West Coast, where his dad had moved with his other family.

His dad answered on the second ring, his voice hushed. "What do you need?"

A part of Carter wanted to hang up because it wasn't as if he had something to talk to his dad about. Calling him had been a mistake. Carter pinched the bridge of his nose. "I just wanted to let you know where I'm at these days, since I moved. I'm in Texas now. I can get you the address, if you want."

"I only have a few minutes. We're heading into Austin's favorite restaurant to celebrate his upcoming graduation."

A stone settled in Carter's stomach. Of course his dad would be busy celebrating one of his stepbrothers—the family he was proud of. He had ditched Carter and his mom for them, after all. Because of that, Austin and Brooks had known a completely different upbringing than he had. Carter did the math in his head and realized Austin would be graduating college in May and no doubt he would be graduating debt-free on account of their father paying for everything, whereas Carter was drowning in school debt. The same father who had purchased a vacation house in Turks and Caicos, while Carter was living out of a little old lady's garage trying to scrape together enough money to pay for books for the next semester.

Carter ground his teeth together. At thirty years old, he shouldn't still care about his father's favor or approval and yet here he was. No matter what Carter did, he would never be good enough for his father. Because he would never be Austin or Brooks and nothing else would ever matter about him but that, as far as their father was concerned. He shouldn't have called.

In fact, he should let go of the desire to connect with his dad altogether.

Dad cleared his throat. "Calling and not saying anything—this is odd behavior, Carter. Even for you. Are you on drugs or something?"

His shoulders tensed. "How can you even ask that?"

"Your mom had been known to dabble and I know that poor excuse for a husband of hers was a full-out druggie."

"Well, I've never touched the stuff." That or alcohol. Not after seeing what a monster both vices had turned his stepfather into. "Do you think I could have made it through veterinary school high, Dad? Come on."

"So it's about your school again, is it? If you're trying to guilt me or get a loan from me to pay off that school debt, then you have the wrong number, son. If you had chosen to be a real doctor then maybe—but animals? Carter, I don't know where I went wrong."

It had probably been when the man had walked out on his wife and twelve-year-old son to start a new family with his much younger mistress. Or before then, when he had constantly belittled his mother until she had the self-worth of an amoeba, which had left her prey to a man like Carter's stepfather. But Carter knew saying any of those things would only garner him caustic words from his father.

No wonder Carter failed at every relationship he ever attempted to have. His own father didn't care about him—why should anyone else?

Carter rose and turned toward the hay bales. He fisted his hand. "I've never asked you for anything."

His father let out a humorless laugh. "Correct me if I'm wrong here, but I remember you showing up on my doorstep unannounced, asking for a free ride."

Carter closed his eyes and let a breath rattle through his chest.

He had been eighteen when he had showed up at his dad's house. Eighteen and homeless after his stepfather had beaten him to a pulp and kicked him out of the house. All that his biological father had seen when he opened the door were the bruises and broken skin, so he had assumed Carter was getting into fights at school.

He had pegged Carter as the aggressor and used his wounds as evidence to support his theory that Carter would be a bad influence on the sons he was raising in his new, perfect family. His father had moved his new family to California soon after that.

Carter's shoulders caved forward and his voice wavered. "That was almost thirteen years ago. I was just a kid. I was a kid and you turned me out."

His father made a half-exasperated sound. "You were troubled and I couldn't have you around Brooks and Austin. They were small and impressionable. You know that."

"And their big brother might have tainted them, is that it?"

"You're a grown man," his dad said. "You need to get over the past."

"Oh, I'm over it, believe me," Carter practically growled.

"Well, as fun as this has been, I have to hang up. I need a few minutes to go over the speech I'm giving for your brother. He got his degree in accounting and already has interviews lined up, and he hasn't even graduated yet. We're very proud."

Carter might never call his dad again after this conversation. It had only served to reinforce his belief that no one cared about him or his problems. No one would ever want to love a beat-up version of a person that his own parents hadn't even been able to care about. This was why Carter had chosen to work with animals—they didn't have pretense and they loved without needing to know if he was *worth* loving.

Carter hung up and spun around to sit down but he froze when his eyes met Shannon's. She stood five feet away from him, her eyes wide.

Carter's heart rammed against his chest. No one was supposed to know about his sad past, least of all one of the Jarretts.

He cleared his throat. "How much of that did you hear?"

Shannon's breath caught the moment Carter turned around. Despite the night's chill, his cheeks were flushed. His arms were shaking and his chest was visibly rising and falling with jerky breaths. If he had been anyone else, she might have been afraid with the way he looked that he was about to yell at or hurt someone, but instead, everything about him screamed that *he* was hurting. And that made her heart twist. Her fingers itched to smooth away the deep frown line on his forehead. She wanted to do something to help ease the pain he was so clearly experiencing.

"Enough." She wound her fingers together. "Your dad?"

Carter's gaze went to the ground and then moved to the other side of the barn, away from her. His Adam's apple bobbed. "I hope you're really thankful for the family you have in there." He gestured in the direction of the main house.

"I thank God for them every single day. I know what I have isn't the norm for many people." Shannon took a step closer. "You're really upset. Will you tell me what's wrong?" She touched his forearm but he flinched and turned away. Shannon knew how blessed she was to have brothers who would do anything for her and parents who had showed their love for her in a million different ways. Not everyone had that sort of upbringing. Her heart went out to Carter. If he had been one of her brothers, she would have been hugging him already.

But Carter definitely wasn't one of her brothers.

Gathering her courage, Shannon wrapped her fingers around his bicep and eased him gently in her direction so she could meet his eyes again. "Family doesn't have to be blood," she said. "We're capable of building our own families through friendships, especially as adults."

Carter's laugh dripped with bitterness. "I tried that once." He dropped onto a nearby hay bale, moving out of her touch again. "I'll spare you the sob story and just say it didn't go well."

Hay dust skated through the air, illuminated by the barn lights buzzing above them. Shannon studied the scars along his cheek and jawline, the ones she had thought made him look like a rugged cowboy the first day they met. Today they elicited her sympathy. Despite the warm personality he had displayed and the encouragement he so readily offered, Carter was a man of many scars. Both inside and out.

She fisted her hands to keep herself from reaching out to touch his face. Fisted them against whoever had hurt him, as well. Sucking in a fortifying breath, she sat down next to him, leaving a few inches of space. She waited a heartbeat before asking, "Do you want to talk about it?"

He shook his head. "Not now, not ever."

On Carter's other side, Wing Crosby swung his head up and drowsily waggled his beak. He let out one long honk. Carter ran his fingers down the gander's back and Wing leaned into his touch, acting more like a puppy than a bird.

Carter cleared his throat. "Did you know when they're in a flock and one goose gets sick or injured or if one is shot, two others leave the flock and follow that one to the ground? They will stay with the injured goose to protect it and make sure it's fed until either it's better or it dies. But whatever is going on, they don't leave one of their own alone or unprotected." He petted Wing Crosby again. "For all the irritating honking, they're incredibly loyal creatures."

Shannon knew he was trying to change the subject and maybe she should have let him. But the man she had overheard speaking with his father had been heartbroken and she wanted him to know she was there for him. She could be there for the Carter who wanted to spew facts about animals or the Carter who was in pain. Whatever he needed.

She let her shoulder rub against his. "I'm sorry someone hurt you," she whispered.

He exhaled a long puff of air and finally relaxed against her. "I'm fine."

"Clearly, you're not," she said gently. "And that's okay, Carter." She tilted her head to make eye contact with him. He was turned her way, leaning in so he was only a breath away. "I hope you know it's completely normal to not be okay. It means you have a heart. That you're human." Her voice shook a little. "But I know what it's like to think you're damaged goods that no one could ever love. I get it, if that's how your dad makes you feel."

"You're wrong," he whispered. "About the damaged goods part." His eyes searched hers. "Because you're very easy to care about, Shannon." She moistened her lips. If he kissed her, she knew she wouldn't pull away. The spicy scent of the cologne he wore wrapped around her as she leaned a bit closer.

Suddenly, Carter straightened and jolted to his feet. "I have to check Tater Tot." He started to cross to the row of stalls. Wing Crosby shot to his feet, too, and shook his tail in an indignant way.

Shannon trailed after Carter. "What's wrong with him?"

At the first stall, he reached toward the tan horse inside. "Colic," Carter said. "He was pretty bad earlier. After I turned the rest of the herd out to pasture, I gave him a dose of Banamine. It's a fairly strong painkiller, so his discomfort level seems to be down, but he's not out of the woods."

Shannon edged closer so she could pet Tater Tot, as well. Her fingers traced over his velvety muzzle. "He was my first horse when I was little. I used to ride him every day after school. I'm the one who named him. Well, he came with a different name because he was four when my dad bought him, but I switched it."

Tater Tot made a waffling noise as they petted him. She noticed a bucket of water in his stall.

Carter grinned for the first time that evening. "Well, young Shannon gets an A-plus for naming in my book.

I've worked at my fair share of ranches and so many horses have boring names. I can tell you this is the first Tater Tot I've ever met."

"I was all of five when I got him, if that. He's the same color as a tater tot and they used to be my favorite food, so really it was quite an honor for him." Tater Tot moved away from them and pawed the ground. Shannon knew colic could be really dangerous. They had lost horses to it quickly in the past. "Did you call Spira?"

Carter made a face. "Give me a little credit. I went on hundreds of colic calls during school—it's probably the most common callout for horses. Besides, I looked at Tater Tot's records and he'll be twenty-five this year. So surgery is out of the question. I've already given him medication, so at this point there isn't much else the doctor would do."

"I've heard you're not supposed to give a horse water when they have colic." Shannon motioned toward the water bucket in the stall.

Carter turned and leaned his back against the stall. "Professionals are split down the middle on that one." He shrugged. "In my experience, water helps. You need liquid for your body to work, right? And it absorbs elsewhere in the body, not just the intestines." He rolled at his shoulder so he was angled toward her. "If he was making weird noises when he was drinking or if he started wheezing, then of course we'd take it away. For now, he's doing well."

"But what if he gets worse?" Shannon had grown up at the ranch and knew enough about horses to know that if Tater Tot's gut twisted he wouldn't make it. Carter was right about him being too old for surgery. It was far too much money and too big a risk to take on an old trail horse they only used for campers.

Carter pushed off the stall door and made his way toward the office, motioning her to follow. "I'm going to stay up with him in the barn all night to make sure he doesn't." When he opened the door to the small office the strong smell of bitter coffee wafted out. "Want a cup?" He glanced over his shoulder.

"Sure." She followed him into the small room.

"Fair warning." He pulled two mugs from a deep drawer. "It's the leaded stuff."

"Good." Shannon fished some creamer cups out of the same drawer before accepting the coffee from Carter. She dumped four creamers and two packets of sugar into the steaming drink before taking a sip. "Someone has to keep you awake."

He set his mug down and cocked his head. "You don't have to do that, you know. I'll be fine on my own. I can drink the whole pot." He tapped the coffee maker. "And I can always make more if I need to. I won't let anything happen to Tater Tot, if that's what you're worried about."

After the pangs of loneliness Shannon had felt around her family earlier, she didn't want to head back to her bunkhouse. All that waited for her there were more reminders that she was alone and might always be. She wanted Carter's company right now.

Maybe she needed it.

And maybe—just maybe—he needed her company, too.

Even if he wasn't willing to admit it.

Chapter Six

Carter was finishing his second cup of coffee when he heard Tater Tot start to roll in his stall again. Discarding the cup on the nearest perch, Carter rushed down the hallway, flung the stall's door open and dropped to his knees beside the horse.

"Oh, no, you don't." Carter grabbed the horse's halter, preventing the animal from rolling again. He wasn't about to let Shannon's childhood horse hurt itself or worse. He would have been out here with any horse from Red Dog Ranch, but now that he knew this one was special to Shannon, he only wanted to double his efforts to save it.

Behind him, Shannon skidded to a stop in the hallway. "What can I do?"

"Grab a lead." With a few encouraging words and prods, Carter guided Tater Tot to his feet and brought him out of the stall. Shannon thrust a lead line into Carter's outstretched hand. He clipped it onto the horse's halter. Tater Tot plodded down the hallway for a few steps and then stopped to paw at the ground. The horse tossed his head wildly.

Carter placed a hand on his neck. "Hey, now. You're okay. You're going to be okay," he murmured to the horse until it calmed down. Carter glanced at Shannon as he jutted his chin toward the barn door. "Can you open it for me? I find they stay calmer if they're walked outside."

Shannon nodded and jogged ahead, unbolting the wide door and rolling it open enough for Carter and Tater Tot to walk out.

"Make sure Wing stays in there," Carter said. The bird was liable to waddle after them into the night and become coyote bait.

"Until you showed up here, that bird used to follow me everywhere," Shannon said. "Now I'm chopped liver to him."

Once they were safely outside, she rolled the door back until it was almost closed and then fell into step beside Carter.

At well past midnight, drapes of darkness swathed the fields. Shannon tugged the zipper on her hooded jacket all the way to her neck and then hugged her middle. A sharp wind tore over the ranch, causing the tall grasses and new flowers to roll and toss like an angry ocean. Carter pulled his hat down a bit to make sure it was securely on.

"You know," Shannon said, jamming her hands into her jacket's pockets, "if we had a riding arena we could be walking him inside right now. Let's keep that in mind for encouragement while we're planning the horse show."

Carter laughed. "True, but then we'd miss the stars." There were thousands of them out right now. Tiny pinpoints of hope against the darkness. Individually they seemed insignificant—not enough to matter or make a difference against the vast night sky—but together they were enough to light their path.

Shannon latched onto his arm, stopping him in his tracks. She looked up, her mouth wide-open. "I haven't been outside this late in a long time. It's beautiful." Her whispered words held the weight of awe.

As he watched her, Carter's heart pounded loud and hard in his chest. His mouth went dry. He wasn't sure he had ever seen anyone as beautiful as Shannon Jarrett before. And yes, with her blond curls and wide eyes, he found her physically very attractive, but it was so much more than that. Despite all she had been through, Shannon was kind and brave and warm and always ready to smile. And being around her made Carter wish he was strong enough to be all those things, too.

I'm sorry someone hurt you.

Clearly, she had overheard the bulk of his phone call with his father. From his side of the conversation, he was sure she could have heard enough to understand some of what had gone on. And she definitely knew by now that his upbringing wasn't the bright one she must have had.

Most people probably would have turned and fled after hearing his exchange with his father. As riled up as his dad had gotten him, Carter must have looked frightening when he ended the call. Yet Shannon hadn't run off or even blinked at how he was acting. In fact, she had stridden right up to him and reached out.

Tater Tot huffed but lumbered forward. They needed to keep him moving.

Carter cleared his throat. "Are you warm enough? I'm going to have to walk him for a while, but if it's too cold just say the word and we'll do a loop to drop you back home, okay?" While he didn't find the night too cold, Shannon very well might. And some distance was bound to help his heart. It would definitely be safer than having her near enough that he could drink in the caramel and vanilla scents that always trailed her. He hadn't even known her long enough to feel like he was losing himself—but Shannon hadn't hesitated about hugging him when they first met. She had gone out of her way to be kind. And she had clung to him when she needed protection, had looked to him for encouragement with something that was incredibly important to her, and had walked toward him when he was hurting instead of walking away.

Where Shannon was concerned, Carter was in very real danger.

"You're not shaking me that easily, cowboy." She looped her arm through his again. "Besides, who's going to protect you from the mountain lions if you're out here all alone?"

This time he didn't even attempt to fight the grin that washed over his face. "I can count on you to protect me, huh?"

She straightened her spine and rolled her shoulders.

"Oh, yeah. No one gets to mess with my buddy Carter." She reminded him of the Cowardly Lion in *The Wizard of Oz* as she put up her fists. "Not on my watch." She called into the darkness, "Hear that, cougars? Don't even try because Shannon's got his back."

He scrubbed at his jaw. "You realize they lived in plenty of the other places I've been?"

She blew her hair out of her eyes. "Sure, but haven't you heard everything's bigger in Texas? That includes mountain lions." She elbowed him in a joking manner. "Face it, you need me."

Maybe he did.

Carter shook that thought away. Shannon was his boss's sister. All things considered, she was probably more off-limits than Audrey had ever been. Back then, he had been a lonely teenager making mistakes, but he was a man now and knew better. Knew that it was up to him to keep others safe…that his lot in life was to never connect, never have anyone too close so that he couldn't hurt them. He still remembered all the horrible things Audrey had yelled at him. He had ruined her life. Just like his mom's. Just like Amy's.

He already cared too much about Shannon to chance causing her pain.

But he couldn't deny how good it felt to have her cuddled against his arm as they strolled through the night. They could walk together to help Tater Tot, couldn't they? There was nothing wrong about that.

Shannon finally broke the silence. "So I realized earlier that even though we've been talking a lot, you've shared surprisingly little about yourself."

His gut clenched. He kicked a small rock in the path, making it skitter into the field. "Is that so?"

"You're really good at making it seem like you're being open when you're not at all." She gently jiggled his arm. "I'd like to know something about you. Something real. If you're willing to share."

The whole point of taking a job at a remote ranch in Texas had been to keep himself unconnected. Make good money for a year or so, have very few expenses, stay around animals and then get out before anyone could care enough to miss him. Or more likely, before he missed them.

But Shannon's nearness made warmth flood his chest and he hadn't felt like that in a very long time, if ever. He didn't want to drive her away, not tonight. If he had to he could always pull away tomorrow.

Carter licked his lips. "What do you want to know?"

"On the phone—" She looked out across the field and then back at him. "So you have siblings? Would you tell me about them?"

Last time he told someone everything about his past she had called him *trash* and sent him packing. But Shannon wasn't Audrey and he knew not to tell people everything anymore. No one needed his life story, but he could share a little here and there. Safe things. Rattling off information about his siblings should be fine.

He shot out a long breath. "Like you, I have three siblings. But the dynamics are a bit different. I'm the oldest."

She squeezed his arm, letting him know she was there. She was listening.

But already he wasn't quite sure where to start without getting too deep. He would have to talk about the divorce and touch on what a horrible person his father was. Even without saying too much it was difficult to avoid that part.

He would say it fast and just plow through all the information at once. "My parents divorced when I was twelve but by then my dad already had a four-year-old son with the woman who's now his second wife. That was Austin and she was pregnant with Brooks when my dad left."

"Your poor mother."

"She took it hard, even though I've gathered she knew he had a mistress and another family for years before they finally split. I think she thought that if she just ignored it, it wouldn't be true." He laughed once, but it held no humor. "She was wrong."

He kept Tater Tot's lead rope so the horse couldn't reach the grass. Letting a horse with colic eat would undo all the good the walk was doing.

He squinted at the stars, doing math in his head. "That makes Austin twenty-two now and Brooks eighteen." He thought about the fact that his dad had been busy celebrating Austin when he had called. Did they make fun of Carter when his dad got off the phone? How foolish they all must have thought he was. His throat felt tight suddenly. Maybe he was allergic to some of these Texas flowers. "I'm not close to them."

"Their loss," Shannon said in a matter-of-fact way.

Carter shrugged because he wasn't certain she was right. Of course, she was being kind. But he had always considered being shut out from that side of the family *his* loss. They all had good lives and were cheered on by their parents whereas he wasn't.

Since he was this far into the mess that was his family, he might as well tell her about all his siblings. "Then there's Amy. Amy and I aren't actually related by blood. My stepdad is her biological dad and her mom passed away when she was still a baby. She was seven when my mom married her dad. That would make her almost twenty-six now if I'm calculating right."

"So, around my age," Shannon said.

Carter glanced her way.

Her hip bumped into his as they turned down another beaten path in the field. "From the way your voice changed while you were mentioning her, I'm guessing you and Amy are close."

"More so when we were young." Back when she used to run to his room to hide when their parents were fighting. When she knew to go into his closet and lock herself there for safety, even if he wasn't home. For a while, they had been best friends. Then he'd gotten kicked out and she had been left to handle both of their parents on her own. "But we haven't been close for a long time."

With a gentle tug on his arm, she pulled him to a stop. "Do you believe in God, Carter?"

Carter scrubbed his hand down his face. "I'm a Christian, yes. But not the church type." He blew out a long stream of air. "That probably sounds horrible. I don't mean it in a bad way. I love God but the church and I have had our differences."

She tucked her hands around his arm again and they

started walking. "I'm not going to judge you for that. God meets us where we're at. He's spent the last few years patiently pursuing me when I was making horrible choices. While of course I believe we should be a part of a church community, the act of attending church doesn't make someone a Christian. Where their heart is does." She took a deep breath. "Maybe I'm going out on a limb, but I think God brought you here for a reason. And I think He wants to do something in your life and use you to impact other people. But you have to be willing to let that happen, Carter."

Shannon was kind, but Carter knew better. He was no one's blessing from God. He never would be.

His fingers tightened on the lead rope. "Let's not get carried away. I'm just here to make an honest dollar so I can pay down my school loans."

"Well, you can brush off what I said, but you've impacted my life already and that's something you can't just shrug away."

Uncertain how to safely continue navigating the conversation, Carter swallowed hard. He refused to hurt Shannon but they were already heading down a road that could end badly if he didn't switch directions with her. If they got too close. If he let himself get invested and decided to stay… She deserved so much better than a man like him. He needed things to shift back to safe ground—topics that didn't involve emotions and declarations.

Tater Tot hadn't tossed his head, pawed at the ground or attempted to lie down to roll the whole time they had been walking, so Carter veered them back toward the barn. The building was dwarfed by the distance they had created by walking for so long.

They made it halfway across the field before he felt Shannon fidgeting beside him. Despite his recent thoughts about not wanting to risk getting any closer to her, Carter couldn't suppress his smile or his curiosity. "Out with whatever you want to say."

Shannon groaned. "Am I that obvious?"

"The silence was killing you, wasn't it?"

She tossed back her head and laughed. "It was excruciating. I'm not used to holding back."

Since their very first encounter she hadn't been one to bite her tongue. He enjoyed when people were that way. Then at least he knew what he was in for. So it struck him as strange that Shannon hadn't come right out and said something. Had she taken his silence to mean he was upset? While he might have been confused and conflicted, he definitely wasn't upset.

Carter caught her gaze. "Remember what I said the other day about being heard? That goes with me, too, Shannon. You can say whatever you want around me." He ducked his head to meet her deep brown eyes straight on. "No fear, okay?"

"Right," she said. "Well, I just wanted to ask you about being a veterinarian. I mean, you have your degree, right? We should be calling you Dr. Kelly."

"If you haven't figured out by now, I'm not much for titles."

She nodded in a thoughtful way. "Why would you pick to be a head wrangler when you could be running your own practice?"

He rolled his shoulders. "It takes a lot of money to set up a practice." Money he didn't have and wouldn't have for a long time. "And I have eight years' worth of school debt that needs to be paid off. So it seemed smarter to try to pay those loans down before taking on another huge financial hardship."

They were close enough to the barn now that she released her hold on his arm and made her way to the barn door. Some of the warmth from earlier drained from his body. Maybe it was colder at night than he had given Texas credit for.

She dragged the rolling door open. "Couldn't you join an already established practice?"

He led Tater Tot into the barn but stopped in the hallway, waiting for Shannon as she secured the barn door. "You're right, I could." And he had, initially, but the head veterinarian had been driven by numbers, booking appointments on top of each other so none of the doctors had time to provide quality care to the animals. The rush had led to mistakes. Carter had left after a misdiagnosis on his part led to a family pet having to be euthanized. Besides, after growing up under the thumbs of his father and then his stepfather, the thought of placing the control of his career into someone else's hands didn't sit well with him. "There are a couple of things I hope to do before settling down, so that's a part of my choice, too."

"What type of things?" She passed him and held open the door to Tater Tot's stall.

Carter chuckled, shaking his head. "You're just full of questions tonight, aren't you?"

She rolled her eyes.

He unhooked the lead rope from Tater Tot's halter and left the horse in his stall to rest. Hopefully, they had worn him down with all the walking and the gelding would fall asleep and wake up on the other side of his bout with colic.

Carter looped the rope over his shoulder. "There was this overseas study program with Veterinarians Without Borders offered my last year at school. They travel all over the world and care for animals in remote places. You get all sorts of hands-on experience with rare animals and illnesses. It's a once-in-a-lifetime opportunity." He might as well tell her why he didn't end up doing the program. Because this was Shannon, after all, and she would ask if he didn't come right out and tell her. "You needed supporters for the program and I wasn't able to raise the funds, so I didn't get to go." He fiddled with the end of the rope. "Dr. Spira did give me paperwork for another similar program the other day. It's a Christian organization where you go on a three-month-long veterinarian mission trip and assist people with their animals but also talk to them about God. They're accepting applicants for an Africa trip and a South America trip."

Shannon lifted the rope from his shoulder. "That sounds like a great program. You should apply." She hung the rope on a peg along the wall. He hadn't realized he was following her so closely, but when she turned around they were only inches apart. Her breath caught, and in what must have been a reflex motion, her hands came to rest on his chest. She looked up at him, meeting his gaze, and she didn't pull away. "You deserve to chase after your dreams, Carter. I get the feeling no one's ever told you that."

He had only ever dreamed of making something of himself, but here, with Shannon so close, that dream suddenly felt small and insignificant. For thirteen years Carter had kept his heart safe. By focusing on school and the future he had avoided relationships of all kinds. Because if life had taught him one thing, it was that he was better off alone.

But her words had made him light-headed for a second. Or maybe it was simply how long he had been awake and the amount of caffeine buzzing through his bloodstream that was making his head spin.

Tired. That was all this was. And nothing more.

Shannon absently shoved chicken pesto pasta around on her plate. She couldn't stop thinking about everything she and Carter had talked about while they were taking care of Tater Tot last night. And not just talking. She had a suspicious feeling that they had come close to kissing at least twice.

What was going on?

After what she had endured with Cord, she wasn't ready for a relationship. Honestly, she didn't know if she would ever be able to trust her heart again. And certainly not with a man she had only just met and who she had to pry personal information from. Carter was her friend.

Just a friend.

He was helping her plan the horse show because

Rhett had asked him to, not because he wanted to spend time with her. Any more, people didn't choose Shannon when they had free time—not her brothers or their wives, not her friends from church, because she had lost them all while dating Cord.

And certainly not Carter.

After all, *she* had imposed on his time at the barn last night. Not the other way around. Hearing about his past had made her feel closer to him, but she had to remember that she had all but forced him to tell her those things. It wasn't as if he was readily offering information. And Carter hadn't gone out of his way to know her.

No one cares about what you have to say.

Everyone would be disappointed if they knew the real you.

She pressed her hand to her forehead. Any almost kisses she thought had happened were in her imagination. Shannon laid her fork down, her appetite gone.

In the past few months, she had thought about joining a support group for survivors of domestic violence but hadn't done so yet. Maybe it was time. She had the number for a local group in her bunkhouse and she would call them today. She wanted better mental and emotional tools at her disposal so she could cleave and separate out Cord's voice and the lies he had fed her from her own thoughts. She wanted to be healthy. Not for Carter—they had only just met and he probably didn't think of her as anything beyond his boss's annoying sister—but for herself. She wanted to be well and whole and if a man did come along someday, she wanted to be ready. She wasn't right now, but she could be if she did the work and healed.

Thickness coated her throat and she blinked rapidly. She hadn't felt a surge of hope this strong since she realized Rhett had made it through the tornado last year.

Shannon and Carter had plans to distribute flyers for the horse show in town together tomorrow. He had confessed that he was decent at drawing and was supposed to get the design to her this evening. Perhaps she would go back to her bunkhouse and sneak in a nap before then.

She stifled a yawn.

Wade dropped onto the seat beside her and poked her in the ribs. "You slept through breakfast and have yawned your way through lunch—what gives?"

Seated across from them, Rhett lifted his head, clearly listening in on their conversation. As head chef, Cassidy was busy in the kitchen and Rhett had told them earlier that Macy was at home resting. Due to her pregnancy, she had been very tired recently.

Stifling another yawn, Shannon laid down a fork. "Tater Tot had colic, so Carter and I stayed up to take care of him." She stretched her arms. "I think that was my first all-nighter since high school." She yawned again. "Feeling my age today."

Wade closed his eyes and put out one of his hands. "Hold up." He opened his eyes, his brow lowering. "The head wrangler? You spent all night with him…alone?"

Of course her brother would jump to the absolute worst conclusion. "Um, the horse was there. And Wing Crosby and Sheep and Romeo, too."

Wade's frown deepened. "Animals don't count in this equation." He swung in his seat so he was facing her. "Listen, I love you, Shannon, but we don't know this guy beyond his credentials and he could have done anything—"

"Carter is a good guy," Shannon said, cutting off whatever he was about to say. Wade was usually the most patient and understanding of her siblings, but he had stood shoulder to shoulder with her in the trenches when she broke up with Cord. He had seen the worst of it, so of course he would be hyperaware of any potential threats to her now. She loved her twin so much but she wanted him to know he didn't have to worry about her. By now he should know he would be the first person in the family she would run to when she needed help.

"He seems decent so far, but we've been burned by staff members before." Wade snapped his fingers. "Are you hearing this, Rhett? She spent the night alone with your new wrangler." Rhett's eyebrows rose as Wade kept talking. "What all do we know about him?"

Elbows on the table, Rhett pressed one of his fists to his lips. "We verified his credentials and work history and he had to be fingerprinted since he's working with juveniles."

Wade tapped the table. "Couldn't we have Donnelley do some checking?"

Jack Donnelley had grown up in the foster system and during that time Red Dog Ranch had been a big part of his life. Their father had personally mentored Jack and he had often been treated as a part of the family. In the last year, Jack had become one of Rhett's best friends. If Shannon remembered correctly, Jack was now a sergeant in the aircraft operations division for the Texas Department of Public Safety. A lot of words to say he had the means and ability to do some checking as long as he had signed permission allowing him to do so. And everyone who worked for Red Dog Ranch signed the form saying that clearance checks could be conducted on them if the need arose.

Covering her face, Shannon groaned. "You guys, don't. Just please, don't. Carter is only a friend and you have nothing to worry about."

Wade pried her hands away from her face and gave them a gentle squeeze. "I don't ever want to see you hurt like you were again."

"I'm a big girl, Wade." Shannon slipped her hands out of his hold. "I can take care of myself."

"I know you can." Wade nodded. "But that doesn't mean I still can't look out for you. Shannon," Wade said, leaning forward. "I will always look out for you. For the rest of my life. That's my job as your twin, your brother and your friend. I care about what happens to you and I'm going to be worried about any guy you hang around."

How was it possible to want to both hug and throttle her brother at the same time? He was so sweet but he was also making her doubt herself.

Rhett sighed heavily. "Carter is a great employee but I don't know how he is on a relational level. We just want to make sure you're being careful with your heart, Shannon. Carter is the first single guy we've hired here since your breakup with Cord."

"I broke up with him nine months ago. And Carter... Carter's a great guy. He's the first person outside family who has helped me find my strength after everything." She hadn't felt more confident in herself and her choices since long before Cord Anders entered her life.

Wade and Rhett exchanged a worried glance.

Rhett sighed. "Your strength is yours, Shannon. You don't get it from some guy."

"I *know* that." Sometimes talking to them was like running up against a brick wall. She wished Boone was home because he was more rational. He wouldn't jump to the same conclusions as Wade and Rhett. "But sometimes we need to be reminded. Isn't that the whole reason why God says we're supposed to live in community? So when we're struggling or doubting something, a friend can point us in the right direction and remind us about what is true?" She stressed the word *friend*.

It was high school all over again. They might be well-intentioned, but she wasn't a kid any longer. Their protective-bear mentalities had ruined all of her friendships with guys when she was a teenager but she wasn't about to let them wreck whatever tentative relationship was beginning between her and Carter.

Now would have been the perfect time to follow Carter's advice and tell them exactly how their actions made her feel, but she chickened out at the last moment. Wade and Rhett loved her and they would never hurt her. Besides, when she did finally get up the nerve to have that conversation with them, she wouldn't have it in the middle of the dining hall surrounded by other staff.

Shannon shoved up from the table. She wanted to run to the big house and talk to her mother. Growing up, she'd found that their mom always had the best advice. If Shannon told her everything about Carter, Mom would know exactly what to say.

Shannon reeled back around, her gaze directed at Rhett. "How's Mom today?"

Rhett rose slowly. "Regarding that, there's something I need to talk to you about. Wade already knows."

Shannon's gaze ricocheted between her brothers. "Wade already knows what?"

Rhett motioned for her to follow him outside. Even with his much longer stride, she kept pace beside him. Rhett cleared his throat. "Mom's getting worse. These last few months—her decline has been sharp."

Shannon nodded. Even with nurses on staff to care for their mother, Shannon knew the situation was a lot for Macy and Rhett to handle since she lived in the big house with them. Any more, her bad days far outnumbered the good ones and she had recently become an escape artist, slipping away from her nurse to wander the ranch. Even with a GPS watch she wore that linked to an app on Rhett's phone, their mom had wandered into dangerous situations.

"What are you trying to tell me?" Shannon hugged her middle.

Rhett rubbed the back of his neck. "Wade and I think it's time to consider moving Mom to a memory-care facility. Somewhere that's better set up to provide a safe place for her."

The muscles across her back tensed as she worked

her jaw back and forth. "Are you sure this is about what's best for Mom and not about what's best for you?"

"Shannon." Rhett flinched and lowered his head. The action made Shannon want to take back her words.

But she was tired and her emotions were running high. Her voice shook a little. "Because first you shoved me out of the house I've lived in my whole life. And now you think it's best for Mom to be moved elsewhere conveniently when you have a baby on the way."

"I'm sorry if I made you feel that way." He met her gaze with a long, pained look before finally breaking eye contact. "But that's not fair. You know I want what's best for her and I want what's best for you, too."

"Being in her home is what's best for her, Rhett." Rhett reached out but Shannon sidestepped him. "I have to go. There's a lot to get done for the horse show."

Rhett ran his hand over his jaw. "We'll talk more later. I love you, Shannon. I love you so much."

Shannon jammed her hands into her pockets to keep Rhett from noticing her arms were shaking, and then she headed to her bunkhouse. She knew he loved her and she loved him, but love didn't mean she couldn't be upset with him.

Minutes ago she had been filled with hope, but it was quickly trickling out of her. Sadly, hope was like a balloon—beautiful when full and floating, but easily busted and guaranteed to leave a person deflated in the end.

Chapter Seven

The next day, Carter discovered that the Spiras were an animated couple who had recently celebrated their fiftieth wedding anniversary. When Carter had told Dr. Spira that he and Shannon were going to be in town, the vet had insisted on them coming over for dinner.

Carter and Shannon had spent the afternoon entering every business in town to let people know about the upcoming horse show, see if they were interested in signing up for a vendor booth and asking permission to hang a flyer in their storefront windows. Much of Stillwater was now effectively wallpapered with advertisements for the horse show.

After they arrived, Shannon had stayed in the kitchen with Dr. Spira, but Carter followed Mrs. Spira into a wide sitting room. A rich, super sweet aroma wafted through the air.

Carter sucked in a lungful of the delicious scent. "Whatever you guys are cooking, it smells delicious. Thanks again for having us."

"That would be Paul's pecan pie. He's won the blue ribbon at the county fair for that recipe four years running." She leaned forward in a conspiratory manner. "But don't tell him I told you that. It'll go to his head and he'll start making pies every week." She put a hand to her chest. "And I love pecan pie as much as the next person, but a body gets tired of eating the same dessert all the time."

"I think it would take me a long time to get sick of something that smelled that good."

"Give it fifty years and you just might." She grinned, letting him know all the teasing was good-natured. It was clear she loved her husband. She gestured toward a wall of photos hanging above a blue couch. "All my grandchildren." She folded her hands. "Most of them live near Galveston. I so wish they were nearer."

"Have you ever considered moving?"

She sighed. "Paul would have to give up the practice first, of course."

There must have been sixty different framed pictures on the wall. Carter leaned closer. A photo on the edge had Dr. and Mrs. Spira and five grown-ups, all with their arms around each other. Carter assumed those must have been their children. A large picture in the middle showed the doctor and his wife surrounded by seventeen kids.

"That one's old." She came up beside him. "There have been two more since that photo was taken and we have another grandbaby on the way."

Every single picture showed children happy and loved and thriving. What would it have been like to grow up in such a family? His life could have been so different. Carter's throat burned. "You have a beautiful family."

"I've been incredibly blessed." She touched his shoulder. "Paul says you two have been talking on the phone each day. I think it's lovely."

Carter ducked his head. Since their first meeting, the doctor had been calling him each day under the guise of discussing interesting cases he thought Carter could learn from. But each talk turned into speaking about other things, too. While Carter had never felt comfortable opening up to someone his own age, the older man had treated him in a grandfatherly way that had loosened Carter's lips. He had ended up telling Spira about his family and his upbringing. Carter had also confessed to him that he lacked both the funds and the confidence to start his own practice at the moment. And Spira had listened to everything without any judgment in his voice.

Their easy conversations might have been what had propelled Carter to call his father the other day. If he could talk so effortlessly to a veritable stranger, then it stood to reason that he should be able to have a meaningful relationship with his own father.

How wrong he had been.

Mrs. Spira bent near a large potted plant, checking its soil. She glanced over her shoulder. "Has Paul mentioned yet that he grew up in an orphanage?"

Unsure if he was supposed to sit or stand, Carter chose to stand. "He hasn't."

She rose and dusted her hands on her green slacks.

"He was the thirteenth child in the family and by the time he was born his parents already had too many mouths to feed. People did that in those days." She moved to the other side of the couch to check another plant. In fact, now that Carter was paying more attention he realized the room was bursting with potted plants and a few small trees. "I think that's why he's so fond of Red Dog Ranch and stops by there so often. Y'all are doing the Lord's work there."

Carter crossed his arms. "I just keep the horses running."

She looked back at him and smiled. "I'm sure you do so much more than you'll ever know."

Carter swallowed hard. Shannon had said something similar the other day.

"From what Paul has shared, my upbringing was very similar to yours," Mrs. Spira said. "I hope you don't mind that he's told me. We pray together each day and you have been on our hearts."

"I—ah." Carter coughed a little. The image of the elderly couple praying for him caused a wave of emotions to crash over him. "I don't mind at all."

She pursed her lips as she picked up a watering can that had been tucked near the end table. "Back in my day women weren't valued how they should be. You understand when I say my parents weren't kind people. They ended up forcing me to marry a man who would advance their lifestyle without much concern for how he would treat me. I almost died by that man's hand, Carter."

Carter sank into a stiff chair. "I'm so sorry."

She nodded and poured some water into a potted tree. "Paul had loved me since we first met. He waited for me. He prayed for me. And when my first husband abandoned me, Paul was there, ready to marry me. Marrying a divorced woman was frowned upon back then, but Paul didn't care. And despite the lives both of us were handed, we've done pretty well for ourselves." She motioned toward the wall of photographs. "You're a smart man, so I'm sure you know I'm not speaking of his practice or this house."

"It's amazing to hear what you both overcame."

"We've led happy, full and good lives because we chose to live that way." She set down her watering can to cup a leaf on the tree she stood near. "Look how well this tree is growing. Would you believe I grew this from a cut branch?" She ran her fingers over the sapling. "If you couldn't tell, I'm a bit of a gardener."

Carter chuckled and looked around the room. "I noticed as much."

"You can cut a branch off certain varieties of trees and plant it. With the right patience and care that little branch can grow its own roots and become a mighty tree." She shook a finger at him. "Many gardeners will tell you that a branch-grown tree will flourish better than one grown from a seed. These are some of my first attempts and they're doing well. It's all about finding a good branch." She walked away from the tree and stopped in front of Carter. "Something tells me you're the right kind of branch, Carter." She clucked her tongue.

Shannon popped her head into the room. "Dr. Spira says food is ready."

"Come and get it while it's delicious," the doctor called from the kitchen.

Mrs. Spira glanced at Shannon's retreating form and then grinned at Carter. "God can use you to start a new family tree, one that's beautiful and strong without the seeds your parents left you. Do me a favor and promise you'll give what I've said some thought."

He put his hand over his heart. "I will, I promise."

Thoughts of trees followed him into the kitchen, and for the first time in many years he enjoyed a meal around the table with people who felt like a family he would have loved to be a part of.

A few hours later, as Carter and Shannon headed down the front stairs of the Spiras' house, Carter offered Shannon his arm. It had rained while they were eating dinner, and sometimes treated wood could be slippery.

Or so he told himself.

The welcome smell of damp earth surrounded them. Carter sucked in a deep breath. Rain always reminded him of new beginnings—the mess of the old washed clean. Growing up in the North, he had always heard that Texas was very hot and dry. Now that he was living in the part of the state called the Hill Country, he knew that couldn't have been further from the truth. Everything was lush and green here and it rained plenty.

The Spiras had outdone themselves with dinner. Carter was stuffed with the slow-smoked beef brisket, sesame slaw, tortilla soup and pecan pie the older couple had made. They were quite the team, and watching them interact had caused his chest to ache for the new family tree Mrs. Spira had talked to him about. Long ago, Carter had convinced himself that the best thing for him would be to be alone, to not start a family. With the examples he had, what did he know about being a good husband or father? But the Spiras hadn't had role models, either, yet they had raised a large, loving family.

At Red Dog Ranch he had a clean slate and what he did with that was up to him. He had never believed that he was worthy of a future like the one Mrs. Spira had painted for him, but tonight he found himself wondering if maybe worth had nothing to do with it. Perhaps his energy would be better spent on hope than worry.

While Carter had enjoyed the Spiras' company and the meal, he had noticed that Shannon had been more reserved than usual. In fact, she had been pretty quiet in the car and when they were passing out flyers.

Clouds wisped across the sky as the sun began to set, leaving a trail of pink-and-orange light. At the bottom of the stairs Carter stopped. He had to say something— even just to start a casual conversation. Shannon keeping to herself didn't sit well with him.

"I don't know if I've eaten that much at once in my whole life."

Shannon rested a hand on her stomach. "Me, too. When the Spiras keep spooning food onto your plate, it's hard to say no."

"What do you say we go for a walk before heading back home?" He laid his hands on his own stomach for effect. "I could stand to burn off some of those calories."

Shannon's lips twitched. "Hardly."

The downtown area of Stillwater wasn't large but there was a small park on the far end with a bricked sidewalk, flowers and plenty of benches. He led her in that direction.

Just like she'd done the other night, Shannon kept hold of his arm as they headed down the sidewalk. She nodded at a few passing people and waved across the street to a large family.

Carter chuckled. "You know just about everyone in this area, don't you?"

She sighed. "One of the hazards of living in the same place your whole life."

"If you asked me a month ago, I would have said that was a bad thing," Carter said.

She bumped her hip into his. "You're warming up to Texas more than you thought you would, aren't you?"

The smile on her face was the first real one he had seen all day—seeing it made him breathe a little easier. Or maybe it was just that being around her instantly put him at ease, regardless of what the circumstances were. Whenever he spotted her, the same thought hit him: Shannon was stunning. No matter what she was doing or how she was dressed or what her expression was, she had quickly become the most beautiful person he had ever been around.

She was still staring at him when he realized a few minutes had passed on their walk and he hadn't responded. Was he warming up to Texas? "Ah, you could say I'm warming up to lots of things. Must be the Texas effect." He winked. Why had he said something like that? And winked. He wasn't usually a winking sort of man. But being around this amazing woman was messing with his head in ways he had never experienced.

Carter steered her down a meandering path in the park. "You've been quieter than usual today." Trying to figure out if he had said or done something to upset her, Carter thought back to the night they had stayed up taking care of Tater Tot and the couple of times they had seen each other since.

"Just a lot on my mind, you know?"

"I don't know, but if you want me, I'm here and listening." He motioned toward a bench and she nodded, taking a seat.

She slumped against the back of the bench. "For starters, I joined a group for survivors of domestic abuse. My first meeting is tomorrow."

He wanted to celebrate her news but she seemed so down. "I'm really proud of you for doing that." He kept his voice calm. "Are you nervous about it?"

She shrugged. "I know it's a step I need to take. And I want to take it. It's just a change, you know? Putting it all out there. But that's not what has me in a funk. It's other things like what if this horse show is a big failure? Or we set the place on fire by accident? Or… I don't know… Insert something horrible."

Hoping to offer her a semblance of comfort, Carter set his hand carefully between her shoulder blades. "For now, let's focus on the things we can control instead of a bunch of hypothetical situations." He felt her take a deep breath under his hand. He kept talking. "Every single business we stopped in let us hang our signs and a handful of them already committed as vendors. Those are both check marks in our win column today."

"And Violet Byrd returned my call." Shannon swung her head toward him. "She's willing to attend the event, be a judge for the costume contest and run the barrels. She said she's getting ready for the summer circuit and could use the exposure ahead of time anyway. She's even bringing her horse."

Carter assumed Violet was the championship barrel racer Shannon had mentioned the other day. "That's great news, and by my count, that brings us to three big wins today. So what has you so worried?"

She scuffed her shoe along a crack in the sidewalk. "What if I begged Rhett to let me do this and no one shows up and I end up looking like an idiot?"

"Shannon, look at me," he said gently. She angled her head in his direction but didn't meet his eyes. Slowly, Carter touched the soft skin of her neck and lifted her chin. She shivered when he made contact and in a moment of vulnerability he almost lost himself and kissed her. But that wouldn't have been right. He was trying to encourage her as a friend and wasn't about to muddle something as important as her understanding how wonderful and strong he thought she was. Besides, he wanted the best for her and that wouldn't ever be him.

Carter's voice was soft. "Whatever happens, none of the people who matter will ever think you're an idiot for being brave and trying something new. How could they, Shannon? You're strong and you care about people and you've been hurt but still put your heart into everything you do. Anyone who knows you is already proud of you. I sure am."

"Carter," she whispered, her eyes searching his. "How do you do that? How do you say the exact thing I need to hear? It's as if you have this direct line to my heart." She tapped his chest.

He dropped his hand into his lap. "I'm just stating facts."

She eyed him and bit her lip as if she wanted to argue.

He cleared his throat. "Was there anything else on your mind?" A part of him hoped she told him that *he* was on her mind, but deep down he knew that wasn't a conversation that could ever happen. His long-term plan didn't include Red Dog Ranch. Nothing could happen between them, no matter how much he enjoyed her company. "Not that I'm saying that wasn't enough to worry about." He scrubbed his hand down his face. "What I meant was you've been quiet all day and I just want to make sure you're okay before we head back."

Shannon gripped the edge of the bench on either side of her and looked at the horizon. Then she tipped her head up and blinked rapidly.

Was she... She was crying.

Carter's mind spun. "Whatever I said, I'm sorry."

Her lips formed a grim line as if she was holding everything in and she shook her head.

"It's not that." Her voice wobbled. "You said everything right. You always do. It's just, my brothers are thinking of moving my mom to a memory-care facility and I don't want them to take her away." She turned her watery gaze toward him and it twisted his insides to see her hurting. "But I don't want to be selfish and keep her here if that's not what's best for her, either."

Carter hadn't met Mrs. Jarrett yet, so he didn't know how she was doing medically. All he knew was that Shannon was hurting and he wanted to be there for her.

"I lost my home and my dad. I've lost a lot of my independence, most of my confidence and my feeling of safety, and now I feel like I'm losing my mom, too." A mournful sob escaped her lips, the sound tearing at Carter's heart. Without thinking, he wrapped his arms around her. She pushed her head against his chest as her arms went around his back, fingers digging into his shoulders. Then she cried long and hard as he held her.

"I'm so tired of everything getting taken from me," she said against his neck. "Every single time I think I have this little piece of hope to hold on to, it's gone just as quickly. And I know I'm being silly. I know my mom needs more devoted care. But it hurts, Carter. It hurts to let go."

He tucked her hair behind her ear and then cradled her head. He would hold her for as long as she needed him to, even if it made his heart ache for the things he could never have. All the encouragement from Mrs. Spira's earlier words shriveled up inside him.

Because he couldn't have Shannon in his life.

Not like he wanted her.

Not when he would end up being something else walking out on her someday. He refused to be another piece of stolen hope in her life.

Chapter Eight

"It's the perfect day for this." Shannon rolled up the sleeves of her button-down and then put her hands on her hips, surveying the work that needed to be done on the fencing. The sun was out, the ground was dry and the wind was minimal—ideal painting weather. She turned her face up to the sunshine, loving the warmth. Carter might grumble about the heat, but she couldn't wait for summer to roll into Texas.

With only a week until the spring horse show, Shannon had decided that the corral where the event would be held could stand to be spruced up. She, Carter and Easton had spent chunks of time during the last week scraping the old flaking paint off the fencing, and now it was time to give the whole arena a fresh coat. Rhett, Wade and Piper had all joined in and were stationed on the other side of the large oval arena. They had already begun to paint. This half was for her, Easton and Carter to take care of.

The day after they had dinner at the Spiras', Shannon had set up an online sign-up for the horse show and entries were steadily trickling in. Many people had used the comment section on their entry form to say they were excited Red Dog Ranch was doing something new. A few others had simply used the entry form to donate money directly to the building fund, writing in their comments that they weren't going to compete but still wanted to offer their support.

Wing Crosby honked from his perch on top of one of the fence poles. He kept his eyes on Carter as the man lugged a few large cans of paint out of one of the ranch's pickup trucks. Next, Carter hopped back onto the tailgate to fish for a bag of paintbrushes that had rolled deeper into the trunk.

With zero reservations, Shannon watched him. From the first time she had taken notice of him, she had known he was incredibly handsome—and in his Wranglers and a T-shirt that fitted him almost too well, Carter Kelly was near impossible to look away from.

But his looks weren't the only reason Shannon couldn't get him out of her mind. Carter was a good person and being around him made her feel as if she could accomplish anything. She thought back to their walk in the park after their dinner at the Spiras' a week ago. He had been able to tell that there was something bothering her and had cared enough to find out what it was. And once he knew, he hadn't tried to fix all her problems or write off her worries. Instead, he had listened and been there. Having grown up with all brothers and then after dating Cord, Shannon was used to the men in her life rushing in to solve any perceived problems.

For once, it was refreshing to find a man who, by his actions, showed that he believed she was capable. Carter assumed she could handle herself and if she couldn't, then he trusted her to ask for help. She knew if she asked him for advice about anything he would give it, but he would never barrel in and tell her what she should or shouldn't do unless she wanted him to.

Nearby a plastic bag rattled. Shannon swung her attention to Easton right in time for him to hand her a paintbrush.

Carter latched the tailgate back up. Then he walked to the fence line and scooped Wing Crosby into one of his arms. "I'm going to go lock him in the barn so he doesn't get into mischief while we're painting." Wing laid his head on Carter's shoulder, nuzzling his neck a little as he talked.

Easton chuckled and shook his head. "That dumb bird is like your baby."

Carter wrapped his other arm around Wing's body, holding him more securely. "This gander has the brainpower of a peanut. I'm convinced he'd get himself killed every day if one of us weren't watching out for him."

Shannon stepped forward and ran her fingers over Wing's head. "Aww, come on, Carter. We all know you're fond of him. And it's clear that Wing loves you, so don't fight it."

After Carter answered their teases with a long-suffering roll of his eyes, he trudged back to the barn with the goose tucked against him. While he stowed Wing Crosby safely away, Shannon and Easton pried open two cans of paint.

"I'll head down that way." Easton waved his arm, indicating the bend on one of the arena's edges.

"Got it." Shannon nodded. "Carter and I will do this straightaway." She shielded her eyes and squinted to the opposite side, where Rhett, Wade and Piper were working. "And it looks like they've got that side managed. If we keep at it without too many breaks, we can have this tackled in a few hours."

Easton nodded. "Mr. Rhett said they were about to head for a quick break. They've been out here painting for a while already."

A few minutes later Carter joined her. He grabbed a paintbrush and they shared a can, bringing them into close proximity. His elbow bumped hers and their shoulders brushed a few times as they worked. The air between them sparked with a tension neither of them had given voice to yet. A part of her wanted him to grab her and kiss her right here in front of everyone and just be done with it already.

Then again, maybe it was all in her mind. Carter had been at the ranch for a few weeks and he hadn't asked her out or made any blatantly romantic advances the whole time. She wished he would. Shannon wasn't sure if she was ready to date yet, but she knew she didn't want to miss out on getting to know Carter better, either.

"You know," Shannon said, her hip bumping his as they painted. "We never got to have that Bing Crosby movie night we talked about. If you're free tonight, I have plenty of them already at my place."

Carter stopped painting. "I thought you said you

were going to plan a staff party. Invite everyone and put a screen up in the barn."

Shannon shrugged. "That would be better in the summer. We could always watch a few together before then and narrow down the summer choices."

"Let's see how sore we both are tonight before committing to any plans," Carter said. "Painting has a way of finding all the muscles you forgot you had in your body and wringing them out."

He hadn't taken the bait, so the tension was definitely all in her head.

She noticed Rhett, Wade and Piper heading toward the barn to take the break Easton had mentioned.

Shannon ducked away from Carter to work on one of the fence poles.

"I meant to tell you." He slathered paint across a top rung. "I caught one of those old movies the other night. It was playing on regular TV." He squinted over at her. "*His Girl Friday*, maybe?"

Shannon sighed. "You're hopeless, you know that?"

"What?" He froze. A large glob of white paint dropped onto the grass from his brush. "I thought you'd be happy."

Shannon rose from her squat. "That's Cary Grant—who, I give you, is fabulous and far more crush-worthy than Bing in my opinion—but it's not a movie based on Wing's namesake, which was what we were talking out."

"Crush-worthy?" He tilted his head and smirked. "Do explain."

"Oh, you know. Completely gorgeous and super suave. All the things that turn women into fangirls."

She swatted at him. "Don't look at me like that. You know what I'm talking about."

"How about me? Am I crush-worthy?" He waggled his eyebrows, making Shannon even more flustered.

"Oh, please. You know you are." Shannon dipped her brush in the paint again so she wouldn't have to look at his face right then. "Stop fishing for compliments."

A red sports car flew up the driveway, spraying gravel in its wake. It veered off the path, coming onto the grass toward where Shannon and Carter were working. In a heartbeat, Carter dropped his paintbrush, wrapped his hands around Shannon's waist and tugged her out of the way.

Shannon knew that sports car.

It made her sick to remember all the times she had let Cord Anders kiss her in that vehicle or how often he had trapped her in there, hitting the lock button when she had tried to leave. He had filled her head with lies while they drove around at high speeds. He had broken her heart a hundred times over and belittled her in that car, too.

When Cord flung the door open and stomped out, Shannon's mouth went dry and her arms shook. Ever since the protective order had expired, she had assumed he would show up at the ranch one day. But she hadn't fought to have it extended because that would have meant facing him in court all over again. She had hoped she was wrong—that he would move on and never show up here.

Unfortunately, she hadn't been.

Carter's fingers tightened at her waist and she felt his

whole body stiffen behind her. One word from her and she knew Carter could make Cord wish he had never stepped foot on Red Dog Ranch. The knowledge that she had that kind of power behind her, coupled with the two group counseling sessions she had attended, made Shannon stand a little straighter. Cord had made her believe she was without friends, that no one cared and no one would take her side if they knew the real her.

But Carter proved him wrong.

As Cord lumbered toward her, hands fisted and the muscles in his neck already straining, she really wanted to hide. She wanted to hand her problem over to Carter to deal with while she ran away. But she knew if she didn't stand up to her ex at some point, he would keep coming back and she had already learned tools and talking points from her group sessions. She was tired of fearing and looking over her shoulder wherever she went. She was so tired of this man and the control he still wielded over her life nine months after she had left him.

It stopped today.

Cord's lies had deep roots in her heart, but now more than ever, she was committed to yanking them out and watching every single one of the untruths burn in a trash pile. She would not allow him the reins to her heart or mind for even a minute longer.

Shannon patted Carter's hands, a silent request for him to let go. He did so right away. She wanted to re-claim any shred of power she could in the situation. So, although a sick feeling crashed through her stomach and her heart jangled in her chest, she lifted her chin and spoke first. "What are you doing here?"

Cord eased his stance and his lips parted with a slow smile. He had always been good at starting off smooth. "Babe, come on now. Don't be like that. I miss you. Is it so hard to believe I want to see you?"

Shannon sensed Carter behind her. He wasn't breathing down her neck, but he was there. She breathed in, out, in. "I don't want to see you. I want you to leave."

"Can't we just talk?" He made an obvious gesture to mean Carter. "Alone. I just want to talk, babe. It's been so hard without you."

"If you have something to say, you can say it right here in front of present company."

Standing there as Cord made puppy dog eyes made Shannon want to throw up. How had she fallen for this guy? She had to remind herself that he had fooled her a little at a time, not all at once. Abusers never showed their true colors immediately.

Rhett and Wade must have still been in the barn. The second they came out and spotted Cord, they would sprint over.

She clasped her hands together. "But I'd rather you go."

"We belong together." He took a step forward, his nostrils flared. "You know what it does to me to see you with this ape?" He pointed firmly at Carter. "Canoodling on park benches and draped all over each other? It's disgraceful how you let him paw you in public." Cord worked his jaw back and forth. "You shouldn't be with nobody but me."

Cord had spied on them in the park? Did he follow her around often? Had he stalked her for nine months without her knowing? The thought made gooseflesh rise up her back.

Shannon was glad she had her hands together, because if they had been at her sides they would have been visibly shaking. "You are not welcome on our property. And you're not welcome in my life." She tried her best to keep her voice even. "I don't want to ever talk to you again, do you understand?"

"This guy?" He tossed his arm in Carter's direction. His movements were becoming larger and more erratic. "I give him a few weeks tops before he realizes what a waste of space and energy you are." Spittle flew with his words. "He'll take off. Mark my words. He'll wake up and see how annoying and pathetic you are. You were blessed I ever looked your way." Cord thumped his chest. "And you messed that up."

His words aren't true. This was the game of lies he played, but he happened to be really good at the game. Good at sensing what jabs would wound the most. And his shot about Carter not wanting her hit like a blow to the gut. Hadn't she been thinking the same thing earlier?

Carter came up beside Shannon, laying a supportive hand on her shoulder. "I think you've said enough and Shannon has been far more patient listening to your rubbish than you deserve. She has asked you multiple times to leave." Carter's stance widened. "I'm only going to ask you once."

"Don't you—" he shoved Carter in the chest "—order me around." He went to put a hand on Carter again, but

Carter caught the man's wrist and held it. Cord winced before breaking free.

Cord made like he was going to head back to his car, but then he whirled around, eyes wide. He let out a guttural roar. "You like my trash? Go ahead and keep it. She's a weak, worthless piece of—"

"Leave." Carter's voice boomed. "Right now."

Blood thrummed loudly in Shannon's ears. She heard one of her brothers yell from the barn. They would be here in seconds.

Reflexively, Shannon felt all her pockets for her phone before she remembered that it had been missing for two weeks. She yelled, "Someone call the cops."

"Already did," Easton said from nearby. "I called when he first got here."

"You selfish little brat." Cord fisted his hand and swung for her.

But Carter was faster. He threw out an arm, sweeping Shannon to the side, and his momentum placed him in her spot. There was a loud smacking sound when Cord's fist collided with Carter's jaw. Carter stumbled but held his ground. Rhett and Wade were on Cord a heartbeat later, yanking him away from Carter and holding his arms securely behind his back. Cord bucked and spit, but even winded, her brothers were stronger.

Carter straightened his spine to his full height. He scrubbed the back of his hand over his busted lip and then spit blood. It landed close to Cord's feet. In two steps, Carter's stride ate up the distance to where Cord was being held until police arrived.

Inches from Cord's face, he said, "Now, let's get

something straight." The muscles in Carter's arms and across his back were bunched and trembling, holding back all the power he could have unleashed. His voice was ice-cold. "*Weak* is the man who lifts his hands against another person in anger. *Pathetic* is someone who feels powerful when they're belittling others." Carter turned his head and spit another stream of blood. "And *worthless* is a person who finds a sick sort of enjoyment in breaking down and controlling others."

Sirens blared in the distance. The sound finally snapped Shannon into action. She had been frozen since Cord threw the punch.

Surging forward, she looped her hands around Carter's forearm and gently tugged. "My brothers have this. Let's get you some ice."

Carter nodded as he slipped his hand into hers and wound their fingers together. Was he holding her hand to anger Cord or because he actually wanted to? At the moment she didn't care.

She led him toward her bunkhouse and tossed open the door. First she ushered him toward the single love seat sofa that graced her living room and then she headed to her freezer. "Sometimes when there are big swings in the weather I get a migraine and the only thing that really helps is an ice pack, so I have a hoard of them in all sizes," she called from her kitchen.

Carter muttered something she couldn't make out.

Shannon stood in front of the open freezer, letting the frigid air roll over her heated face as she tried to wrap her mind around everything that had just occurred.

Only a week before the spring horse show and her

life was spiraling out of control. She bowed her head and sucked in a sharp breath. *Please, Lord. I feel like every time I'm moving forward, something jerks me backward. As if I'm not allowed to move on because of the mistakes I've made. Help me. Because I don't know what to do anymore—about Cord, about Carter or even about myself.*

Carter touched his aching jaw and winced. His head pounded. That mean dog of a man Shannon used to date threw a pretty good punch. Carter would be feeling that one for a few days.

Shannon sat down on the couch beside him but sideways, so she could face him. "Let's put this on your lip. It's still bleeding some." She handed him a clean rag. He wadded it up and pressed it against the part that hurt. In his experience any injuries on the head bled a lot, making them look much worse than they actually were. After today his lip probably wouldn't be all that bad.

However, Shannon inched closer to get a better look at his jaw. Her warm breath hit his neck and he shivered as her nearness caused his heart rate to spike and his chest to feel tight. She leaned back to a normal distance, only to trace a featherlight finger along his jaw. Carter swallowed hard. He was momentarily afraid his heart was going to pound right through his rib cage. Did she have any idea the effect she had on him? It was a good thing he had a busted lip at the moment because her caress was leaving a trail of fire on his skin and if she had done that when he wasn't a mess, he wouldn't have been able to hold himself back any longer.

He would have been kissing her soundly and thoroughly.

He would have told her that he would take a million fists for her if it meant he got to spend a few minutes with her this close every time.

She frowned, her deep brown eyes full of concern. "That's going to bruise." She lifted an ice pack to his jaw and held it there. The caramel-and-vanilla scent that always lingered around her was strong and Carter absently thought that it was the warmest, most comforting smell in the world.

Still facing him, Shannon laid a cheek against the back of the couch. Carter shifted to better look at her, wedging the ice pack between his face and the couch cushion.

Shannon's gaze tripped along his face until she met his eyes. "I'm sorry you got hurt because of me," she whispered.

Carter tried to smile but doing so tweaked his busted lip so it probably ended up looking more like a grimace instead. "No problem."

Shannon licked her lips. "That wasn't the first time you took a hit meant for a woman, was it?"

He could have brushed the question off or changed the subject. Nothing said he *had* to answer her. But his heart revolted against the idea of misleading Shannon in any way. He found that he *wanted* to tell her the truth—his truth—or at least this part of it.

A slight breeze rustled papers on her kitchen counter. In their hurry, they had left the front door wide-open. Anyone could walk into her home at any minute and

Carter was glad for that thought. It didn't feel right being alone with Shannon in her house when his mind kept wandering to kissing her.

Carter swallowed hard.

"My mom." His throat felt raw as he began. "My stepdad was a horrible man." Carter closed his eyes. A thousand awful memories flashed through his mind. A thousand times he had failed the women he loved. "He beat her within a hair of death so many times and yet she stayed, Shannon." He opened his eyes and met her gaze. "She wasn't strong like you. She stayed."

Shannon placed her hand over his.

His breath rattled. "I used to hide. Me and Amy. We used to hide from them in my bedroom. I could hear my mom screaming and I hid." Would she pull away? Now that she knew he had watched someone suffer and done nothing for so long. "I was a coward for so many years."

"Carter." Shannon kept a hand over one of his but lifted her other to cup the uninjured side of his face. "You were a child." Her thumb brushed along his cheekbone. "It's never the responsibility of a child to fix something like that. They should have led lives that meant you and Amy could have been playing and innocent instead of hiding and afraid. They failed at their jobs, not the other way around." She traced her fingers over the couple of scars along his jaw and chin. "Did he give you these, too?"

As he leaned into her touch, Carter fought the desire to press kisses to her fingertips. He was telling her the second hardest piece of his past and she hadn't run off yet. If he hadn't been willing to admit before that he had lost his heart to Shannon Jarrett, it no longer mattered. He had completely fallen for her and he would do anything for this woman.

He had never felt this way about anyone in his life.

His realization loosened his lips. "I used to get made fun of at school because of my last name. The kids thought a boy named Kelly was hilarious." And he'd been the only Kelly in the family since it was his biological father's last name. "My stepfather found out and treated it as if the kids had struck gold. He used to force me to stand against the brick wall in our backyard as he and his drunk friends made fun of me. They had this game where they would toss beer bottles to see how close they could get it to shatter by me without hitting me directly and I'd get in trouble if I moved or flinched." Carter tapped a scar on his chin. "A few of these are from pellet guns."

"That's horrible." Her tone was a mix of shocked and soothing.

"I filled out my last few years of high school." Carter had spent every afternoon his junior and senior years in the school weight room lifting, focused on bulking up. Knowing he needed to get stronger than his monsters.

Now that he had started, he might as well get to his family's end. "Started lifting. It got to where I could hit back when kids tried to mock me and that stopped them real quick." Carter shifted on the couch. He set the ice pack on the armrest. "At about the same time I started standing up to my stepdad. I'd get between him and my mom and he'd take his anger out on me instead. It made my mom so angry, though. She said it was my fault he

was hitting us. She said I was getting him worked up."
He shook his head.

Shannon stroked her thumb back and forth against
his hand.

"The last time I came home, he was in the middle
of strangling her. I tore him off her and he turned and
came at me in a rage. He ended up kicking me out of
the house that night." A muscle along Carter's jaw tightened and it hurt. "Said he was through with me challenging him. And my mom backed him up." His breath
caught. "She told me it would be better for her and Amy
if I *made myself scarce*." He had been staring straight
ahead, but he turned to meet Shannon's gaze. "That was
thirteen years ago and when I walked out of that house,
it was the last time I saw any of them."

Shannon gasped. "Even your sister?"

His gut twisted at the mention of his sister. Perhaps
he had failed Amy more than anyone else. She was a
kid and he'd walked away. She was helpless and he'd
left her on her own with wolves.

Carter rubbed at his forehead. "She called me two
years ago, when our mom passed away."

"Carter," Shannon whispered. Her fingers tightened
on his hand.

Carter usually did his best to avoid dredging up his
past, so he had forgotten how much it could drain him.
He allowed his head to slump forward. "I didn't go to
the funeral," he said. "At the time, I didn't want to face
Amy." He cupped one of his hands over his eyes and
blew out a long breath. "I felt horrible for leaving her

in that house alone and unprotected. Who knows what she ended up enduring."

Shannon took hold of his wrist and pulled his hand away from his face. "Do you still have her number?"

He nodded once.

"You should call her." She gently squeezed his wrist. "Have you talked to your brothers?"

"That's not fair."

He flipped his hand around in her grasp so they were holding hands instead of her clutching his wrist. "How about this? When you talk to your brothers about how you feel, I promise I'll call Amy."

Her eyebrows rose, but a second later she nodded. "So where did you go—when your stepdad kicked you out?"

"First I went to my dad's house," Carter explained. "At the time he lived in this gated community across town. I rang the doorbell at ten at night and I looked a lot like this." He pointed at his bruised jaw and busted lip. "He took one look at me and said I wasn't allowed in. He assumed I'd been causing fights and he didn't want me around his new sons. Said I'd be a bad influence and I'd ruin them if he let me in. He moved them to California soon after that. I always thought it was to get away from me."

"Oh, Carter." Now she looked like she might start crying. "I'm so sorry."

Pity had always rubbed him wrong. It always would. Not that he believed Shannon was pitying him, but even the possibility that she could be was enough. He wasn't that helpless kid anymore. That certainly wasn't the image of him he wanted her to have. "For all intents and purposes I was homeless for the next few years. I traveled by foot from ranch to ranch and took whatever work I could and slept in a lot of barns. I barely finished high school between it all." Carter leaned his head back and stared at the ceiling. "That's probably enough about me."

Shannon scooted a little closer so she could lay her head on his shoulder. "Thank you for telling me all that. For what it's worth, I think you're the bravest and best person I've ever met."

Except she didn't know everything.

She didn't know the worst of it.

That thought propelled him off the couch. Carter paced away and then stopped with his back to her. He lowered his head into his hands and took a deep breath. He was in love with Shannon Jarrett. The truth of it rocked through him. He knew it like he knew he was breathing. However, he was also aware of the fact that he didn't know how to be a good boyfriend—he wasn't even sure he knew what it looked like to simply be a good friend. If he tried, he would flounder and fail. He would end up disappointing her and he couldn't stand to stick around and see that happen. But loving her had become a part of him and for the first time in his life, Carter wasn't sure he could walk away.

He thought about the application the Spiras had given him for the short-term veterinarian mission trip program. Night after night he had looked over the materials and he had even gone so far as to complete the forms online. But he hadn't pressed Submit yet. Whenever he thought about it he couldn't picture leaving Red Dog Ranch and that scared him more than anything. He was a man without roots—a wanderer—and no person or place was supposed to ever capture his heart.

Yet she had.

This place had, too.

Carter dropped his hands from his face. Was love worth the risk? He had to know if she felt the same way. "Remember that overseas program Spira told me about?"

Still on the couch, she had tucked her legs under herself. "Of course. Have you heard back yet?"

"I haven't applied yet. Do you think I should?" He slowly turned to face her, gripping the back of a chair as he did. "If I got in, it would mean leaving this place. You guys would have to find someone new to work with the horses."

Ask me to stay.

Tell me you never want me to leave.

If she gave him the slightest hint that she cared, he would spill everything. He would go against every promise he ever made to protect himself and be vulnerable enough to chance getting hurt again. He would trust her with the worst piece of himself, the piece he hadn't yet told her about but she deserved to know.

"You can't pass up an opportunity like that. It's your dream, Carter. You *have* to apply. Do it." Shannon pointed at him in a way that made him think of a cross teacher. "Today." She batted her hand in the air. "And don't worry about the horses. Rhett has a file of other applicants from when you were hired. We can replace you in a heartbeat."

He refused to let her see how much one simple sentence had torn at him.

Carter forced a smile. "Right. Of course." A strained laugh slipped out. "I'll submit the application today."

"That's wonderful, Carter." Her smile was bright and wide, and it felt as if someone had punched him in the chest. "It's going to be such a great experience. I can't wait for you to go."

Given how she had treated him in the past, he had wondered about her feelings.

He wouldn't entertain that hope any longer. It had been foolish to believe a woman like Shannon could ever care about him. Even for a second.

He rubbed his hands together. "I should head out. Thanks for the ice." He headed toward the door. "After everything…you've had a rough day. You should stay in and relax. Don't worry about the fence—Easton and I can get it covered."

Once he was outside, Carter opened the browser on his cell phone and logged on to the mission's website. Pulling up his application, he hit Submit and then shoved his phone back into his pocket. It was done. No turning back.

It appeared he might need an early exit anyway.

All his assumptions about Shannon's actions and attention had been wrong. She wasn't growing attached to him. They were coworkers who happened to get along and she was used to being around guys because of her brothers. Carter kicked a stone on the path, sending it rambling through the yard.

We can replace you in a heartbeat.

Thankfully, he hadn't voiced his feelings.

Chapter Nine

The next day, Shannon woke to Rhett and Wade pounding on her door. Yawning, she scrubbed her hand down her face. "To what do I owe this pleasure?"

In the distance behind her brothers, the fencing around the arena glowed white in a wash of morning sunshine. Carter and Easton must have painted it until sundown and she wouldn't be surprised if Carter had already been awake and working to finish the arena today. Despite the chill of the morning, the sight warmed Shannon clear to her toes.

Yesterday after Carter left, she had taken his advice and stayed inside. It had been a good thing, too, because she had finished confirming all the entrants for the horse show and also double-checked with all the booth vendors to make sure her rental orders for the tables and chairs were correct. She had designed some social media ads and posted them on all the ranch's online channels and had written a press release, forwarding it to the local media. She had even forwarded the press release to news outlets in San Antonio. One of the posts on social media had garnered over three hundred comments overnight, and most were people saying they were planning on attending.

"We're sorry to wake you." Rhett's voice snapped her back to the present.

Wade waved a file folder. "But you need to see this and it couldn't wait." He brushed past her. Rhett followed, giving an apologetic half shrug as he passed her. Wade dropped the file onto her table, flipped it open and fanned the pages out so most of them were visible.

Shannon rubbed at her eyes. Since she'd just looked at the brightness outside, her vision was trying to adjust back to the dim interior of her house. "What is this? If you guys are trying to drag me into one of those old mystery games we used to play, it's not happening. You two are too competitive so it's not even fun anymore."

Rhett sighed. "That's Carter's criminal history." They didn't usually run total criminal histories for work at the ranch. Since they weren't a long-term living facility, it wasn't required by state law and their father had always believed that people who had made mistakes should still be given a chance. Before working, a staff member had to be fingerprinted, but they only selected histories to be flagged for felony charges or charges dealing with crimes against children. Misdemeanors wouldn't have been noted.

She made it to the table and lifted the first page, but without her contacts, her eyes still hadn't finished focusing. "I don't understand."

Rhett shoved his hands into his pockets.

Wade crossed his arms. "We had Donnelley do some digging." He jutted his chin toward the table. "Carter has a battery charge, a string of thefts and an old restraining order."

The sheet of paper trembled in Shannon's hand as she tried to make sense of what her brothers were saying. But nothing they said fitted the man she knew. "A restraining order?"

Wade tugged a printout from the back of the folder and tapped on it. "Audrey Baker was the protected party. Has he ever mentioned her?"

"Never." Shannon put her hand out, bracing herself against the table, but her legs still wobbled. She sank onto one of the kitchen chairs. "But these are all old, right? Nothing is recent?"

"Battery and a restraining order, Shannon." Wade tugged on his hair. "The writing is pretty clear. This is Cord Anders 2.0."

Rhett rolled his shoulders. "I'm afraid there's more." He glanced at Wade, who only nodded. So Rhett continued, "Seven different people have reported items missing or stolen at the ranch. All the items have gone missing in the month since Carter's been here. And every missing item was last seen near Carter or the horse barn." Rhett straightened his hat. "It's too big of a coincidence, especially in light of all this." He gestured toward the table. "We at least have to question him about it."

This had to be a mistake.

There was no way Carter had been stealing from everyone.

Then again…she'd misjudged a man before and it had cost her dearly.

Gripping the edge of the table, Shannon looked back and forth between her brothers. "What are you saying?"

"We're saying the man's not welcome here any longer," Rhett said. In an instant he went from concerned brother to formidable ranch owner. "We were on our way to tell him we strongly suggest he turn in his resignation, but we figured we'd speak to you first so it didn't come as quite a shock for you."

Her eyes burned and her throat felt hot. "Do you have any proof for the thefts?"

Wade touched the file folder. "He has seven theft charges on his record. That's proof enough as far as I'm concerned."

"That's not proof." She snatched the sheets of paper away from him and scanned for a date. Frantically, she flipped through the pages. "These are all mostly from twelve or thirteen years ago. Here." She tugged out the restraining order. "This one is the most recent, from *eleven* years back." She whirled toward Wade. "How can you of all people judge someone's past?" She pushed against his chest. "We only have to go back five or six years to find a longer string of arrests for you."

"I'm not that guy anymore." Wade's frown spoke his hurt better than words ever could.

"Neither is Carter," Shannon said.

Wade spoke slowly, as if he thought she might not speak the same language. "We plan on searching his cabin for the stolen items. Let's just say I won't be shocked if we find them."

"Shannon." Rhett put a hand on Wade's shoulder. "Don't you think it's odd that he rarely stays more than a year at a ranch before moving on? The only time he stayed in the same place was for schooling, but his address history showed he moved frequently even when he was there. Given everything we know, it feels like a pattern."

"But I thought Carter was a good guy," Shannon whispered. Moments from the last few weeks crowded her mind: Carter coming to her rescue with Cord more than once, and him encouraging her to reconcile with her brothers. She thought about the fact that every time she had confessed fears or worries to him, he had spent time building her up and telling her how strong she was. That wasn't the behavior of an abuser.

Confusion was making her wish she had ignored the knocks on her door and stayed in bed. She pressed her forehead into her fingertips and groaned.

An arm came around her shoulders. Rhett. He pulled her gently into a hug. "It's going to be okay."

Shannon had spent her life looking up to her eldest brother and she found he was almost always right. But this time she wasn't so sure.

Wing Crosby's honk was full of indignation.

Carter chuckled. "Well, buddy, if you had just stayed where I put you instead of being a little escape artist, we wouldn't be in this mess now would we?"

Last night Carter had set his alarm to wake up at four in the morning so he could finish working on the fence for Shannon. He wanted her horse show to be a success and if painting the riding arena was important to her, then he had been determined to get it done on schedule.

Of course Wing had gotten out of the barn and come looking for him like a lost puppy. The goose had brushed against wet paint and nestled next to a fence pole dripping with paint before Carter had noticed him. Subsequently the faithful bird had gotten his feathers covered in paint, which Carter knew wasn't good for him. Geese preened and preening meant Wing would eventually ingest the paint. Carter wasn't about to let that happen.

With Wing Crosby tucked under one arm and bottles of Dawn and Vaseline in his other hand, Carter headed toward the hose, where he had dragged a small trough. But Wade, Rhett and Shannon blocked the doorway to the outside, bringing him up short. Shannon had a manila file folder clutched tightly in her hands and her eyes were red-rimmed.

Carter's heart lurched into his throat. He looked past her brothers, meeting her gaze. "Are you okay?"

Brow scrunched, Wade regarded him. "What are you doing?"

"Wing brushed against some fresh paint." Carter lifted the bird a little so they could see him. "He needs to be washed."

Rhett hooked one of his hands on his belt buckle. "Put the bird down for now. We need to talk."

Carter set Wing on a nearby bale of hay. He glanced back to Shannon and the sight of her in distress tore him in two. "What's going on here?"

Rhett stepped forward. "I've got a string of items

that have reportedly gone missing. Almost all of their last known locations were at or near the horse barn." He pulled the file from Shannon's hands and passed it to Carter. "We also pulled your criminal history. You gave consent as part of your application."

Carter's eyes narrowed. "I remember it said that would only be used during special circumstances."

Rhett nodded gravely. "I would consider this circumstance special enough to warrant it."

The battery had been during his senior year of high school. A kid who had bullied him for five years had jumped him in the hallway and Carter had decided enough was enough. One well-placed punch and the kid had been sprawled on his back, crying in the middle of the hallway. It hadn't mattered to the policemen that Carter had been attacked first; by then the responding officers had recognized him as the homeless kid they were always chasing out when he overstayed his welcome in public buildings during winter. They had already labeled him as troubled and were happy to have a reason to justify their label. He wasn't proud of his arrests, but he had only ever stolen things during times he was close to starving. And the restraining order had been Audrey's dad's way of flexing his muscles.

Everything in the file was true. But he knew that file didn't define who he was.

Not that it mattered.

They would run him out of their lives just like the church people in Audrey's town had chased him off in the end. Without asking him—without getting his side of the story—they had already decided who they thought he was. This was what tight-knit communities did and he had been stupid to believe, to hope, that Red Dog Ranch would be immune to such behavior.

They had decided he was trash.

He needed to leave.

Carter worked his jaw back and forth. "So you've gone and decided I'm the thief, then?"

Shannon reached toward him. "Tell them you didn't do any of those things."

In the end, his extra hours of work and dedication hadn't mattered to the Jarretts. The honorable way he had acted with their sister hadn't mattered. They had still judged him and found him lacking. Telling them he hadn't stolen a thing in more than ten years wouldn't matter. He could explain until he was blue in the face, but they had already passed judgment on him, so no, thank you. He would retain his dignity and walk away.

Leaving was the only power he still had in the situation.

The only power he had ever seemed to have.

Carter yanked the barn keys out of his pocket and tossed them to Rhett. "I suppose I won't be needing those any longer."

Rhett caught the keys. "Thank you for doing the right thing."

He swallowed the response that rose to his lips. Arguing with people who thought the worst of him wasn't worthwhile. Carter would leave and they wouldn't miss him, but first he would make sure the animals that needed immediate care got it. Carter pointed at Wing.

"Someone needs to wash him with Dawn until the

paint is gone. Dab Vaseline on his eyes before you start, though, so the suds don't hurt them." He thumbed in the direction of the nearest stall. "Sheriff blew an abscess this morning. I just finished soaking it in Epsom salt but someone needs to pack his hoof with antibiotic and wrap it. I'd tape over it because he's not one to stay still." Carter bumped Wade's shoulder a little harder than necessary when he pushed by him to get out of the barn.

Shannon shot past Carter and skirted to a stop in front of him, blocking his path. Her eyes were wide and a little wild as they searched his. "You can't just leave."

He looked away, off toward the field, because the sight of her upset did funny things to his heart and made him want to reach toward her. Which was the last thing he needed to do right now.

She grabbed his arm. "You're just going to leave Wing like this?"

Carter slipped out of her touch. A quick glance over his shoulder confirmed his suspicion—both her brothers were only a few feet behind them, watching everything. "I need to go."

She swiped at her eyes. "He's bonded to you, Carter. You can't just walk out on him."

He had to go. He had to make an exit before he broke down. Because a part of him wondered—hoped—that she was talking about herself and not about the goose. But that was the type of wishful thinking that would hurt him the most. Hadn't Shannon told him he would be easy to replace? That she couldn't wait for him to go?

The memory of her words finally propelled him into

motion. Shannon calling after him only caused his feet to stumble twice on the trek back to his bunkhouse.

One good thing about having so few belongings was he could vacate a place in record time. Although, by the time Carter reached his bunkhouse, his legs were shaking. Leaving this place felt different. His gut clenched as he shoved things into his duffel bag. For a month this had been home—not just a place to live, but a real home.

Getting out was for the best, though. He had let himself get carried away, falling for Shannon. His heart was too involved and leaving would save him that. Save him further pain.

At least that was what he told himself as he drove out of the driveway and turned onto the street, Red Dog Ranch getting smaller and smaller in his rearview mirror.

Chapter Ten

"And don't you forget to water all my plants." Mrs. Spira hugged Carter. She gave great hugs—tight but not too tight, and she held on long enough to show she cared but not too long to make things awkward. She let go, but only to step back and settle her hands on his shoulders. "I'm especially worried about a little apple tree I planted in the back a few years ago, so keep an eye on it. It may look scrawny and it hasn't given fruit in the three years I've been growing it, but I believe it has good roots and its season is coming. It'll bear fruit when the time is right and until then our job is to faithfully tend it."

Dr. Spira came up behind Carter and slapped him on the back. "She's talking more about you than that scraggly tree and if you know what's good for you, you'll listen to her. She's a smart old bird." He wrapped an arm around his wife and tugged her to his side as he pressed a kiss to her temple.

She swatted at her husband. "Oh, you."

Watching them interact caused an ache to spread through Carter's chest.

Was it wrong to want that?

After leaving Red Dog Ranch he had headed straight to the Spiras' house. On the drive there, Carter had decided that he would come clean and tell them every last piece of his story. Would they reject him like everyone else had? When he arrived, they had welcomed him warmly and sat on either of his sides on the couch, both of them holding his hands as he spilled everything he was ashamed of. Every regret in his life. Nothing sugarcoated.

They hadn't let go.

In fact, Mrs. Spira had put clean sheets on the guest bed and had invited him to live with them for as long as he wanted. Dr. Spira had hugged him and told him how much God loved him and that they did, too. They knew everything, yet they were leaving him alone in their home with all their belongings while they left for a trip to meet their newest grandchild. They hadn't judged him. Instead, they had chosen to believe him and put their trust in him.

It was a first in Carter's experience and he didn't take the honor lightly.

"She's right, you know," the doctor said. "You are like that little tree in our backyard. You love the Lord, Carter. I know it looks different in your life than in the typical church person's but that doesn't make your love of God or your commitment to Him any less true or real. After what you've been through in your life, even an ounce of faith is a huge and wonderful thing. As a

Christian, you have planted roots in God, and as long as you let Him, He will water your roots."

Mrs. Spira nodded along. "There's a verse about it, in the book of Psalms." She went to the pile of bags by the front door and dug her Bible out. "Right here in the very first psalm it says, 'And he shall be like a tree planted by the rivers of water, that bringeth forth his fruit in his season; his leaf also shall not wither; and whatsoever he doeth shall prosper.'" She closed her Bible and smiled at Carter. "That's you, son. If you believe in God and continue trying to walk in His ways, your season of bearing fruit will come in time. Everyone's time is different, so comparing yourself or your spiritual journey to others doesn't work. In fact, it'll only ever hurt us." She hugged her Bible to her chest. "And later in that psalm it says that God will not judge His people. That's you, in case you weren't tracking along." She winked.

Dr. Spira's smile held more fatherly warmth than Carter had ever seen in his thirty years of life. "You are free, Carter Kelly, so stop living under the weight of a judgment that doesn't exist."

Carter's throat burned as he hugged them both good-bye again. It was still burning an hour later when someone knocked on the front door. Not only had the Spiras tasked him with watching over their house while they were gone, but the veterinarian had convinced him to handle all emergency calls at the clinic. It could be anyone.

But it wasn't just anyone.

When he swung the door open, it was Shannon

standing on the front porch. She gave him a soft, slow smile that did crazy things to his heart.

Carter gripped the door frame. "What are you doing here?"

"My brothers are wrong about you." She fisted her hands. "I told them that, too. I'm sorry I didn't speak up when they were talking to you yesterday. It happened so fast."

"You have nothing to apologize for," he said. "Everything in that file they have is true, Shannon. There's no pretty way to explain it all away."

"But you didn't steal anything and you're not that guy anymore."

"How do you know?"

"Because I've learned to trust myself again, Carter. And you're the one who helped me have the strength to do that when I didn't believe I ever could. I'm going to figure out who did it and clear you."

Her words made his heart feel as if it was rapidly growing inside his chest. First because he was proud of her strength, and second, because she cared enough to want to clear his name.

"It's enough to know you don't think it's true." He thought about the day he had asked her opinion about applying to the overseas program. When she had told him she was excited for him to go. Could he have read her meaning wrong? Because after this conversation it didn't feel as if she wanted him to leave.

Her gaze captured his and didn't waver. "Is it okay if I kiss you?"

Shock washed through him and he stuttered a few times before getting out, "Why would you want to—"

"Yes or no. It's not a difficult question."

He gulped. "It's more than okay."

With no other encouragement, Shannon stepped forward and put her hands low on his chest. She slid them to his sides, letting her fingers trail up his arms. He kept his hands to himself for the time being, wanting her to have the lead, the power to keep things going or abort whatever it was she was doing. Even though every cell within him screamed to touch her.

Carter's breath shuddered along with his body. "You're killing me."

She just smirked, her eyes sparkling, and she brought her fingers to his jaw and drew his face down to hers.

Their lips were only an inch apart when Carter pulled back. "This isn't a good idea. I have a past, Shannon."

She guided his face back toward hers and the scents of caramel and vanilla wrapped around him. "I don't care about your past." Her lips whispered the words against his. She closed the last hair of space and that was all it took for Carter's world to turn upside down. His fingers found the soft blond waves he had wanted to feel since the first day they met. His other hand scooped against the small of her back, drawing her against him.

How could this strong and brave and beautiful woman want him? She came from a good family and believed the best of people. She went out of her way to make sure everyone else in her world was happy and cared for. Shannon was the best person he had ever met. And he was a broken mess who didn't deserve her, but in this moment he didn't care. After what she had endured, Carter knew that her kiss and her trust were the most precious gifts he could have ever been given.

When they finally broke apart for air, he was the one who went right back for another.

The second time their kiss ended, Shannon pulled back a few inches, her hands resting on his chest, and looked up into his eyes. "I meant what I said. I don't care about any mistakes in your past, only who you are now. And the man you are now is pretty irresistible." Her laugh was husky.

It was time to tell her everything.

Carter took one of her hands and led her down the steps. Fingers entwined, he brought her to the Spiras' backyard, which was a veritable nature center. Even though their house was technically in town, it sat on the very edge. Their backyard and side yard touched a forest preserve.

Large rock slabs paved the way for a winding walk around a little pond, tons of trees, flowering bushes and a big vegetable garden. The path meandered all over their acre of land.

"I've told you a lot about myself. More than I've told almost anyone." The Spiras were the only exception. Their reaction to his unburdening gave him the courage to keep talking. "But there's something I need you to know." He paused, glancing at her. "You may not think I'm that great a person afterward."

She squeezed his hand, a silent prod to keep talking. *Where to start?*

Carter sucked in a fortifying breath. After seeing the

Spiras together, Carter knew that was what he wanted for his life. Despite all the roadblocks he had faced getting to that conclusion, he knew he wanted love and a family. To start his own family tree far removed from his childhood experiences. If he held back from telling Shannon the worst of him, then he was also taking away the ability to know real, true love. Love like the Spiras had, which loved no matter what.

Would Shannon still want to be this near to him? He had to find out.

"One of the first things I discovered when I was homeless was that you could often find free food at churches. Whatever town I happened to be in, I would watch for potlucks or Bible studies and attend for the free food." He shrugged, knowing it sounded silly. "I was eighteen and wandering the country when I walked into Audrey's church."

Shannon gasped. "Audrey Baker."

He nodded. "Her dad was the pastor. She figured out I was homeless and took pity on me. When blizzard season hit, she started sneaking me into places at night. At first it was a big game to us, but then she suggested sneaking me into her bedroom."

Shannon's toe caught on a rock but Carter grabbed her before she fell.

He scratched at his forehead and scanned across the pond. "She said she was in love with me, but I think she got a thrill from going against her father more than anything. I thought I had found a home—a forever—but in the end I was only her rebellious phase. Nothing more." He kicked at the ground. "When she realized she was pregnant, she turned on me. Said I'd wrecked her life. She had wanted to go away to college that fall and her parents forced her to postpone it. She told me she wasn't about to have the spawn of some homeless piece of trash."

"Spawn? Trash?" Her whispered words held a note of horror. Shannon touched his shoulder. "That was ugly and horrible of her. But like you once said to me, people's actions reveal who they are, not who you are. I hope you didn't take her words to heart."

Not take them to heart? He had felt like a worthless piece of trash every day since Audrey said those things.

He had to keep talking, to get it all out. "She knew I wanted to travel, but I told her I would settle down, find work and do whatever I could to provide a stable life for both her and our child. My whole life my parents had made me feel unwanted. I didn't ever want a child of mine to feel that way," Carter said. "When I found out she was pregnant—thinking about becoming a dad changed my life. I knew I didn't want to be like my father or my stepfather, so I ended up turning to God for help. I became a Christian during that time."

He laughed once, bitterly. "Even still, she didn't want the child and wanted me even less. I wasn't good enough for them, though supposedly God said I am. Her parents accused me of ruining her. Not that I blame them. That's when they took out the restraining order—they were afraid I would convince her to marry me and raise our baby. They said I'd done plenty of damage already and they weren't going to let me do any more. As if owning up to responsibilities was a bad thing."

Shannon opened her mouth, closed it, opened it again. "What happened to the baby?"

"The baby was stillborn." And he hadn't been there. Hadn't been allowed at the hospital because of the order, so he'd never got the opportunity to have closure or hold his child. Never got to say goodbye. It still hurt. "I know I hadn't originally been planning to become a dad or settle down so young, but something inside me broke when I found out." He touched his hand to his chest as a sharp pain went through his heart like it always did when he remembered his child. "I went to the church elders for counsel and do you know what they told me? They told me that it was a *blessing*." He spit the word out. Even after all these years, his gut clenched at the words and they made his chest burn with anger. "That God was *protecting me* from my sin. They called the death of my child a blessing, Shannon."

She stepped in front of him and drew both of his hands into hers. "I'm so sorry."

"I told them that what they were saying didn't sound like the God I had been getting to know by reading the Bible. And they answered me the same way my mom had the day I left." Despite his effort to control his voice, it wavered. "They said it would be better for everyone if I just left. So I did." He met Shannon's gaze and held it. She hadn't pulled away. "The church people ran me out of that town, so I've never walked into another church since."

"God didn't run you out, Carter. Never attending church again hurts you, not them. It robs you of the chance of being in community." Shannon took a half step closer. "And not all Christians are like that. Don't get me wrong, I'm sure plenty are—there's so much rushing to judgment and the online world only seems to have made that worse—but the people who count will love you and stick by you no matter what."

Love? Had she said *love*?

So spent from dragging up everything about Audrey, Carter didn't have it in him to dig into her use of such an important word. It probably meant nothing. He sighed. "I just wanted you to know. But I haven't… In case you were wondering…" He moistened his lips. "I haven't even kissed anyone since Audrey. Until you."

And if he had his way, he would never kiss another after Shannon.

Shannon's heart had twisted a hundred different times as Carter told her what had happened in his past. She wanted to cry for the young man who hadn't been able to tell his child goodbye and the guy who had been told by the girl he loved that she thought he was total trash. No wonder Carter didn't open up to anyone. Before today, Shannon had been forced to pry information from him, little by little. Now his reservations made perfect sense. It was beyond her understanding how Carter had turned out to be such a kind and caring man amid all he had faced. Between his parents, his stepfather and what had happened with Audrey, he could have been cold and angry.

But Carter had never been anything but warm and compassionate to Shannon. And she had seen him again and again go out of his way to help Easton and the girls in their riding group.

If he had feared that telling her about Audrey would

drive her away, he couldn't have been more wrong. If anything, he had only endeared himself to her more. They had both made some huge mistakes in previous relationships, and they both knew what it was like to trust and love the wrong person. For the person who should have cherished them to wound with words and belittle them.

Now that Carter was done talking, she took another step, bridging the last of the space between them to hug him. The second her arms went around him, she felt his muscles sag, tension releasing. If only she could give him half of the strength he had helped her find since they met. He buried his face between her shoulder and hair as he returned her hug tightly.

"I'm so sorry all that happened to you," she murmured close to his ear. "I'm so sorry for all you've gone through and how people have treated you. They didn't *see* you, Carter, and that's their loss."

Carter shook his head and set her back from himself. "You keep being so nice to me and I don't know what to do with it. I'm not a good guy, Shannon. I'm not—"

"You don't think you're a good guy?" She laughed. "How do you not see yourself?"

A frog splashed into the nearby pond as she waited for Carter to say something.

His brows knit together. "You heard everything I just told you, right? The thefts and the battery—those things really happened back then. And Audrey... I *did* ruin her life. I don't think her parents ever let her go away to school."

"Let's see if I've got this right." Shannon laid a palm

on his heart, savoring the sudden freedom to touch him. She grabbed his hand and drew their joined hands up between them. "You were a teenager who was willing to stand in the way of and stand against physical abuse." She tipped her head up, making sure he was absorbing her words. "You took hits for your mom, Carter."

A muscle in his jaw jumped.

She went on, "At only eighteen you were willing to give up your dreams in order for a child to have the best chance at life—to do better than was ever done for you." She stepped back, getting more animated. "*And* you took a punch for me before you even cared about me." She tapped his chest. "So don't you dare tell me you're no good, when you're the kindest man I've ever met. Your heart is so big and you care so much and you crave justice for others. You've helped me find my strength when everyone else only wanted to baby me."

Shannon brought her hand to his face again. She loved the feel of his stubble under her fingertips. "As far as I'm concerned you're the best guy out there," she whispered.

Carter's Adam's apple bobbed. He looked up, blinking at the sky. "You're wrong." His voice was thick with emotion.

She placed a hand on either side of his face and guided him to look at her. "No, I'm not."

"Well, about one thing." His gaze finally crashed into hers. Looking into his blue eyes was like gazing across the ocean—calming yet full of endless possibilities and hopes. It made her want to dive in, even though she knew there was a risk. "When I took that punch from Cord,

I had already lost my heart to you. I was long beyond merely caring by then." He brushed hair from her shoulder and then leaned in, claiming her lips again.

Shannon's hands found their way to his solid chest and she wound her fingers into the fabric there, tugging him close.

"I want you back at the ranch," Shannon said against his lips. She would do whatever it took to clear his name with Rhett and Wade, though she didn't think it would be that difficult. After Carter had left she had gone over the details pertaining to when the missing items had been reported to have disappeared. A quick check on the volunteer log had shown Easton working during every reported theft and some had lined up to when Shannon knew Carter had been with her in town and Easton had been primarily unsupervised. Which wasn't uncommon. At eighteen he was considered capable of completing tasks without a staff member forever on his heels. She would talk to the teenager and see what he had to say and they would go from there.

Just as Carter was moving to deepen their kiss, his phone started going off. "I'm sorry." He broke away and scrambled to answer it in time. "Spira listed my number in the away message for the clinic. It could be someone having an emergency." But his head jerked back when he looked at the screen. "Why is Wade calling me?"

Shannon snatched the phone from Carter's hand and answered it. "What do you want?"

"You shouldn't be with him, sis." Wade's voice was clipped. "We ran that background check to keep you safe. Does that mean nothing to you?"

Shannon squared her shoulders. It was high time for her to tell her brothers to back off. She should have done it weeks ago when Carter first suggested it. The solid foundation she had begun to build thanks to her group counseling sessions helped her gather her courage. "Is Rhett there with you?"

"He is."

"Put the phone on speaker."

"Done."

"Listen," Shannon started. "I love both of you so much but I don't need you guys rushing in to fight my battles all the time." She reached for Carter's hand. He pumped it lightly in a show of support. "I know you think you're taking care of me and you don't want me to get hurt because of what happened with Cord, but the truth is you're both trying to control me just as much as Cord ever did."

Rhett cleared his voice. "That's not fair."

"It is when you're telling me who I can and can't spend time with." She stepped closer to Carter. "I don't need you guys to be my heroes. I just want you to be my brothers. I just want to know you love me and support my choices."

"We do, sis." Wade's voice was subdued.

"Then let me go. Let me make mistakes or thrive without the fear of constantly disappointing you."

"You've never disappointed us," Rhett said.

"How you both act makes me feel like I do."

Wade sighed. "You're right. We've overstepped ourselves a lot since Cord. I'm really sorry, Shannon. I just—I love you a lot."

"I know you do. And you, too, Rhett. But I need you both to take a step back from my life. I don't need either of you acting like overprotective dads toward me."

"We can do that," Rhett said. "I promise we'll both be better."

"And tell us when we're overstepping," Wade added. "I'm sure we won't go down this road perfectly but we want to be better for you."

Shannon let out a long breath as adrenaline from finally having this hard conversation buzzed through her body. "So we're all okay, then?"

"We're all more than okay." Rhett's voice was warm.

Wade clicked off the speaker setting. "Hey, so totally not being overprotective, but I really do need you to come home."

"Right now?" She glanced at Carter. One of his eyebrows went up in a silent question. Shannon forgot to breathe for a second. With his dark hair, blue eyes, strong build and the trail of stubble across his chin, Carter was gorgeous. There was no other word for it. He was steal-your-breath gorgeous.

And Shannon had just kissed him.

A lot.

"It's urgent." Wade's voice broke her out of her moment of swooning. "We're all meeting at Rhett's and you're the only one we're missing." When she didn't answer right away he added, "It would mean a lot to me if you would head back now. It's a personal thing and I want to share with everyone in the family at once. We even have Boone, June and Hailey waiting on video chat already. But this needs to happen today because

June's heading off on a weeklong trip with some of the women from their church next week."

It's a personal thing. Shannon latched onto Carter's bicep, holding on for support.

Last year Wade had been diagnosed with thyroid cancer. He had undergone surgery and radioactive iodine treatment during his battle and had been declared cancer-free afterward. But he had to go in for checkups every six months and he and Cassidy were always balls of stress while they waited for results each time.

What if Wade's cancer had returned?

Shannon's heart lurched into the back of her throat. Wade was her twin. Growing up, he had been her confidant and best friend. Last summer, his return had been the driving force to finally get her to leave Cord. Despite the fact that he had been fighting cancer at the time, he had walked every step of the breakup with her. From discovering her bruises to filing police reports and facing the man down in court proceedings—Wade had held her hand through it all.

"Of course, Wade. I'll head home now." Shannon hung up with him and turned to Carter, thrusting the phone back at him. "I have to go. My brother. I have to go."

She took off down the steps and was in one of the ranch's trucks a heartbeat later. Carter called after her, but she had to get to Wade.

Rhett showed up at the Spiras' doorstep the next morning, entirely contrite. He explained to Carter that when Shannon had told Easton about Carter leaving over the thefts, he'd confessed to taking all the items.

"And I'd like to know if you would be willing to resume your position at the ranch," Rhett said. "Honestly, the horses have never had better care."

Carter wouldn't return for Rhett's sake or even for the horses. While he had grown to love Red Dog Ranch and believed in their mission, if he went back, it would be for Shannon.

They hadn't spoken since she had rushed off yesterday.

But Carter had a responsibility to Dr. Spira, too. Late last night a frantic client had showed up at the doctor's house, begging him to save their potbellied pig, Ham Solo, who was a beloved family pet. Upon inspection, Carter had discovered that Ham Solo had torn the cranial cruciate ligament in his front left knee. In order to save the pig, Carter had scrubbed up and performed surgery to stabilize the leg. Once he was done, Carter had been exhausted but had only been able to sleep off and on for a few hours in a chair in the recovery room because he had needed to stay near and monitor his patient. Ham Solo would require supervision and care for a few days before Carter was comfortable with him going home. With Spira gone, Carter couldn't exactly leave the pig alone.

"I won't be able to come back today," Carter said. He explained about Ham Solo. "I can probably be back by Friday, since Dr. Spira is set to return late Thursday night." He would want the doctor to be able to have a good night of rest before taking over the care of the pig and any other animals that came in between now and then.

Rhett pursed his lips. "The horse show is Saturday morning."

"I know." Carter jammed his hands into his pockets. He wanted to be there for Shannon's event, but he couldn't simply shirk his responsibilities at the clinic. "I'll work as many hours as she needs me to on Friday in order to be ready to roll on Saturday. I'm not going to let her down."

"I know you won't." Rhett turned to leave, but then he stopped on the steps and turned back around. "She was the one who found out it was Easton taking things. She told me she had a hunch it was him before she sought him out."

"I hope you weren't too hard on the kid." A stone settled in the pit of Carter's stomach. Easton was a hurting teenager who needed direction and mentoring. Being a part of the ranch's volunteer program where he could get hands-on experience for a résumé was vital to Easton's future success. A huge setback now could derail his life for a long time, and from his own life experience, Carter knew that was the last thing Easton needed.

"Nah. But I thought of a great punishment." Rhett's mouth twitched in what looked like it might want to be a grin. "We assigned him to the mentoring program. I told him he needed closer guidance and counseling from one of our best." Rhett leaned a hip onto the rail. "I hope you don't mind that I assigned him to you."

"Me?" Carter couldn't believe his ears. The man who had basically kicked him off his property a few days ago was now saying Carter was one of his best people on staff?

"My brother and I—we messed up, Carter. There's no other way to say it," Rhett said. "We were quick to judge and slow to listen and handled things in a way that was upsetting to both you and to God." He laid a hand on his chest. "Shannon is our baby sister and Wade and I both feel as if we failed her where Cord was concerned." His shoulders slumped as he kept talking. "We just didn't want to see her hurt and that blinded us, and we responded poorly when we got your record check back. We're deeply sorry and ask forgiveness for how we acted."

Carter opened his mouth but nothing came out. No one had ever asked for his forgiveness like that before. It all felt a little strange and overly formal. He closed his mouth, took a deep breath and tried again. "I forgive you and I get it. Shannon's really special."

"She really is." Rhett tapped the railing. "Oh, speaking of that, I wanted you to know why Shannon rushed out of here—"

Carter held up a hand. "You don't have to share family stuff with me." It felt too personal, too much to know about an emergency among the Jarretts. In the end, he was only a staff member.

"It's fine. Wade wouldn't mind because everyone at the ranch knows by now. Cassidy is pregnant. So it was good news." Rhett edged backward down the steps. When his boots hit the sidewalk he stopped and dipped his head, tipping his hat to Carter. "I hope you stick around, Carter. You're good for my sister. I'm sorry I didn't see it before."

After Rhett left, Carter lowered himself onto the front steps and dropped his head into his hands. Carter knew so little about navigating family relationships. Already he felt way in over his head. Did heading back to the ranch mean he was committing himself to something he wasn't ready for? He loved Shannon, but that didn't necessarily mean he was prepared for all that went along with it. If things progressed he would be expected to join their family.

Carter didn't even know how to start processing that thought.

He grabbed the railing and yanked himself to his feet. As he headed back to the clinic his steps were wobbly with exhaustion. For now he would focus on things he did feel confident about, and right now that was taking care of Ham Solo.

Chapter Eleven

Shannon couldn't have picked a better day for the spring horse show. It was the Saturday before Easter and it was hard to believe that only a year ago they had been dealing with the tornado that had ripped through their egg hunt event. This year's egg hunt was planned for next Saturday but was going to be much smaller and only open to local foster kids as opposed to the grand affair of years past, which had been open to the public.

Giant, lazy clouds hung in the sky, playing peekaboo with the sun, and the slightest breeze kept it from feeling too warm. Yesterday a team of twenty volunteers—herself and Carter included—had decorated the ranch, striped the ground to designate the parking area and set up twelve sets of transportable bleachers as well as hundreds of other chairs.

Since Carter had been back they hadn't been able to speak beyond delegating work and asking what else needed to be done. The couple of times she had happened upon him alone he had been on the phone. But she hoped to be able to catch him at some point today so they could talk. She had thought he might flirt with her more openly now, but so far both yesterday and today's interactions had been kept very professional.

The makeshift parking lot had filled within an hour of opening and now Wade was directing cars to park in one of the cow pastures. Chatter filtered through the air as people milled between the vendor booths, and the smells of cinnamon and fried food mingled together beautifully. Shannon's phone, which Easton had returned, buzzed with a message from Macy letting her know Violet Byrd had arrived and was looking for her. As she headed to collect Violet, she sent Carter a message saying he should make his way to the judges' table because they'd be starting in ten minutes.

A few minutes later Shannon slid into the seat next to Carter and Violet took the last spot on her other side. Initially, when they were planning the horse show, Shannon hadn't been able to remember Violet's name, but now that they had been reintroduced Shannon recognized her from the years the woman had attended the summer camp Red Dog Ranch ran for foster children. If her guess was correct, Violet was a few years younger than she was.

Carter leaned over Shannon to shake Violet's hand. "It's great to meet you. I looked you up online and watched videos of some of your runs." Carter whistled. "You and your horse are truly impressive."

Violet blushed. "Thank you so much."

Carter leaned in more, bringing his face inches from Shannon's, but all his attention was on the barrel racer.

"I saw you're ranked forty-sixth with the Women's Professional Rodeo Association. I have to say, I've worked at a lot of ranches so I know a little about the rodeo circuit. That's a huge accomplishment."

"I plan to get that number up higher this year." Violet winked.

Carter chuckled and started to sit fully back in his chair.

Shannon placed a possessive hand on Carter's shoulder. "Carter hasn't just worked at a lot of ranches. I'm sure he knows a lot because he's actually a veterinarian, too."

"Oh, that's wonderful," Violet said, leaning over to smile at Carter. "Maybe after the show you can have a look at Hawken—my horse."

"Are you kidding?" Carter beamed at her. "That horse is a work of art. I'd be honored."

The whole exchange caused a small twinge of jealousy to tiptoe into Shannon's heart, where it crouched in a dark corner there. *Not good enough. He'll lose interest in you.* Cord's words invaded her peace again. She rubbed her temples and growled internally. Her group meeting for survivors of domestic abuse had been helping her learn how to silence the lingering lies.

But with her long blond hair and striking green eyes, Violet was a very beautiful woman, and suddenly Shannon, who rarely cared about trying to impress others, felt a little shabby sitting next to the knockout. Compared to Violet, she was fairly ordinary. Carter's hand came to rest on Shannon's knee, which pulled her from her odd thoughts.

It was just because they hadn't spoken yet. She would talk to Carter and they could make things official between them, and then the unsettled feelings she was experiencing would go away.

She dragged in a long breath. The scents of arena dust, wildflowers, popcorn and a whiff of the spicy cologne Carter always wore turned into a weird but comforting mix of smells. They were Texas. They were home. Everything she wanted—Carter included. When a ray of sunshine pierced through the fluffy clouds above, Shannon closed her eyes, tipped her face to the sun and prayed.

God, with everything that has been happening I haven't prayed in a while. Forgive me. I should have been praying more, not less, when things got hard. Help me weed my heart of all of Cord's lies and from the ones I've planted there, too. This is what I should be doing every time I get one of those thoughts, isn't it? Turning my face toward You, just like I'm doing with the sunshine. I will in the future. I know only Your truth can eradicate them. And, God, please bless things with Carter. Is that weird to pray about? I never prayed about Cord and I know I should have. So...I'm giving over whatever is happening with Carter to You.

Feeling fortified, Shannon turned on the microphone and welcomed everyone. "One year ago, almost to the date, Red Dog Ranch was struck by a tornado. Much of what you see now was leveled and we had to consider closing our doors. But our amazing community rallied around us and helped us rebuild and reopen in time to host Camp Firefly. That's the free summer camp program we run here to serve foster children from all over the state. Because of you, over five hundred children got to spend a week here feeling safe and loved. Thank you for partnering with us today by attending our first ever horse show. The funds raised today will go toward building an indoor riding arena, which we'll be able to use to further expand the programs we offer to kids in need. I really hope you enjoy our show."

The program started with Carter's lemonade relay. He took the stage and gave the introductions. Shannon couldn't hold back her grin as she watched him easily capture the crowd's attention. Cassidy had insisted on making a huge vat of her homemade lemonade for the event even though Carter and Shannon had both explained that a lot of it might end up spilled. However, Cassidy had argued that if the lemonade was fantastic it would be an incentive for people to try harder to get to the finish line with less spills, because when the rider crossed the line they were supposed to down the cup of juice. The event was based on time scores and how much had been spilled, and riders of all ages and skill levels had entered.

Next up was the main part of the show—Shannon's costume challenge. She had gotten a peek at some of the thirty contestants when they were getting ready out of sight, behind the barn, and everyone had gone above and beyond what she had imagined. Nerves jittered through her body as she announced the lineup.

Music pumped through the loudspeakers as a white horse that had been painted with zebra stripes trotted into the arena. Everyone clapped and laughed as the horse's rider, who was dressed like a safari guide, put binoculars to his face and scanned the bleachers. Next came a horse dressed as if he was a doctor in blue scrubs with a huge stethoscope looped over his neck, and his rider wore a hospital gown. The stirrups had been made to look like crutches.

An *aw* escaped from Carter when a little girl riding a huge brown horse clomped into the arena. The tiny rider was wearing a bumblebee outfit and her horse was draped in hundreds of flowers. And the cuteness kept coming—a rider in a Dorothy dress and her horse in a Cowardly Lion costume, Santa riding a dark brown horse that had antlers and a red ball attached to his bridle to look like a nose. The crowd gasped in unison when a giant black horse charged into the judging area dressed like a dragon. His rider had tacked on gorgeous huge red wings that almost touched the ground as the horse marched and pawed the length of the corral.

From her perch at the judges' table, Shannon scanned the crowd until her gaze fell on her family. Front and center, Rhett had his arm slung around Macy, whose hands rested on her very swollen belly. No doubt the bleachers were entirely uncomfortable for an eight-months-pregnant woman, but Macy was tough as nails and no one would have been able to keep her away even if they had tried. Kodiak lay at their feet, her head on her paws. Wade and Cassidy were seated on Rhett's other side. They were holding hands and Cassidy had her head on Wade's shoulder while Piper kept switching from her dad's lap to jumping up and down as she cheered near the fencing. When Rhett noticed Shan-

non's gaze, he lifted his hand in an acknowledging
wave that she returned, but then his wave turned into a
thumbs-up sign. The simple gesture warmed Shannon's
heart more than him writing out his pride in giant sky
lettering could have. Rhett wasn't a thumbs-up kind of
guy. At all. So for him to do that, he was really proud
of her. Wade finally noticed the exchange and blew her
a kiss, then smiled widely.

She mouthed "I love you" to them.

Shannon's heart squeezed. She loved her brothers so
much and always had, but it was really special to feel
as if she was making them proud. Not that she needed
their stamp of approval on her life, but it was nice to
know the people she loved the most in the world sup-
ported her and believed in her.

Blinking back tears, Shannon took the stage again
and announced that rodeo legend Violet Byrd was going
to take the arena with her champion horse to perform
the barrels for their enjoyment. The crowd erupted in
applause and some people rose to their feet, cheering
loudly as Violet and her palomino rode up to the opening in the fence.

A few of the teen volunteers had set up the barrels
and combed the ground while the winners of the costume contest were being announced. Red Dog Ranch
used arena sand in all their dedicated riding areas, despite the fact that it was far more expensive than regular
sand. The added expense was worth it because the an-
gular sand provided better support and safety for both
the horse and rider than normal rounded sand could.
Shannon had taught the barrels to campers before and

they had hosted mini rodeos, but nothing at the speed of what Violet was about to show them.

As the buzzer sounded, Violet kicked Hawken and the gelding burst forward with an enormous amount of power and speed. Sand flew as Hawken's hooves ate up the distance to the first barrel and rounded it quickly. Nostrils flared, he charged to the next one. Violet leaned in, pushing him on as they pounded toward the last barrel. They were moving so fast that Shannon was having a hard time keeping up with their footwork. On the final turn both horse and rider leaned hard—too hard. Hawken lost his footing and slid head-first into the sand, his body crashing down on top of Violet, who was unable to get off him in time. Someone on the bleachers screamed as Hawken tried to raise himself and stumbled directly onto Violet's right leg in the process.

At the same time, Carter flung himself over the fencing and tore across the arena. Likewise, Rhett climbed the fence on the opposite side. Violet attempted to stand but crumbled to the ground with a loud cry. People in the crowd gasped and yelled "No." Rhett reached Violet first and knelt down beside her while Carter rounded up Hawken, secured the horse's reins and calmed him down. The palomino limped badly as Carter walked him slowly toward the exit, turning to pat his neck and say soothing things to the giant beast every couple of steps. While some people might have assumed that Carter should have doctored the animal in the arena, Shannon had grown up around horses and knew Carter could provide better care for Hawken if there were fewer stressors for the horse to deal with. Getting him away from the crowd and into a confined location where he couldn't get himself hurt further was of top importance.

Knees shaking, Shannon turned her microphone on. "Please, everyone, stay calm and keep your seats."

Wade appeared beside her. "Ambulance is on the way."

Shannon relayed that information through the microphone. "For everyone's safety, please stay where you are. We're sorry for the inconvenience."

Rhett strode out of the arena carrying Violet. Macy had rushed to hold the gate open for him and joined them as Rhett walked toward the ranch's driveway. Kodiak led the way, darting through the tall grasses in front of them. Shannon set down the microphone and jogged after the trio. Breath wheezing, Shannon put her hands on her knees as she stopped near where Rhett had set Violet on the tailgate of one of the ranch's trucks.

"I'm so sorry," Shannon finally got out.

Tears streaked Violet's face. "My circuit starts in two weeks. How am I going to ride if my leg is broken? I really hope it's not broken." She covered her face with her hands. "I don't even know if Hawken is okay. I should have asked about him first."

Shannon laid a hand on Violet's uninjured leg. "You don't have to worry about Hawken. Carter has him and he'll take good care of him. We'll take care of him for as long as you need us to."

Rhett cleared his throat. "And don't worry about the expenses. We'll cover all costs as far as Hawken's care and recovery are concerned."

Sirens wailed in the distance.

Violet looked toward the sound but then her chin trembled. She tipped her head up a fraction and swallowed hard. "If I can't race, I'll lose my sponsors."

Rhett glanced at Macy, a silent plea for her to step in. Macy moved forward and took Violet's hand. "Your only worry right now is getting better. You were doing the ranch a favor when the accident occurred and we're not going to abandon you, all right? We'll work something out. You'll see."

Rhett grasped Shannon's shoulder. "Mace and I have got this handled. Why don't you head back to the stage and keep the crowd in order? Wait until about five minutes after the ambulance leaves to start dismissing people to their vehicles." He removed his hand and started to turn away, but seemed to think of something and faced her again. "And, Shannon? This isn't your fault. You planned a really great event that raised a lot of money. Don't let a hiccup in the day distract you from the facts. Accidents are part of life."

The ambulance turned up the drive and a team of paramedics rushed out.

Shannon rounded her shoulders, sent up a quick prayer asking God to take care of Violet and Hawken and then headed to deal with the crowd.

After he got Hawken unsaddled and contained, Carter had called Dr. Spira and asked him to stop by Red Dog Ranch and bring along some of his equipment. Carter suspected the horse had either strained or torn a muscle along with possibly having hurt a tendon, but he wanted a second opinion and also needed Spira to bring medications that the ranch didn't have readily available to manage Hawken's pain.

After administering an anti-inflammatory and helping assess Hawken's muscles, Spira had headed back home to deal with patients at his clinic. But the vet said he would be back first thing in the morning. Carter suspected the man's desire to stop in again so soon had more to do with the fact that Mrs. Spira wouldn't be home until late tomorrow evening than that the doctor thought Carter needed his help caring for the horse. But he would happily accept help, nonetheless. Mrs. Spira was still currently in Galveston helping care for their newest grandchild.

Finally with a minute to himself, Carter glanced at his phone. Amy had returned his call but the voice mail she had left hadn't been too encouraging. In the message she had explained that she had gotten married more than a year ago and had a five-month-old baby.

"I love you, Carter. I really do," Amy had said. "But I don't know if I can reestablish contact with you. I have a family now. And I don't want you entering Emmeline's life only to disappear one day so she's left to wonder what she did wrong to make Uncle Carter abandon her. I know that's not your intention, but I'm a mom now and I have to do what's best to protect her. So let me think about it, okay? I just don't know yet."

It was his third time listening to the message but it still pierced as sharply as the first time. His own sister didn't trust him to be a committed member of a family. She thought he had it in him to make a kid feel abandoned. In her esteem he was lumped in the same category with his mom and stepfather. It would have hurt less for her to slap him outright.

Carter slumped against a wall, letting his back slide all the way down until he was sitting on the floor in the barn. Wing Crosby gave a mournful little honk as he leaped from his perch in the office and headed toward where he was seated. Wing crossed the hallway and settled down beside Carter.

Maybe Amy was right. Maybe he had been fooling himself for weeks thinking he was cut out to be a part of a family—to have even dreamed of the possibility after Mrs. Spira had talked to him about family trees. After all, he was Carter Kelly—the drifter—the man with no roots who wanted to check visiting every country off his list. He'd even told Shannon about his dream to see the world the night they had walked with Tater Tot. He couldn't very well do that if he was tied down. Besides, he had a criminal history and was drowning in school debt. No woman, no family, needed to be saddled with the likes of him.

The door creaked open and Shannon's voice brought his head up. "There you are. I looked for you in about five other places but should have figured you'd still be in the barn." Her smile was so wide and bright it made his chest ache. He loved this woman. He loved her more than he would ever love another person.

But after Amy's phone call he knew the best thing for Shannon's future, the most loving thing he could do, was to not act on his feelings at all.

Sickness rolled through his stomach at the realization. Shannon strode forward until she was directly in front of him. "Rhett called. They're saying Violet has a shattered fibula." She offered him a hand and he took it, rising. "Doctors are telling her it'll take six to eight weeks for it to heal but then since she's an athlete she'll need therapy afterward, before she can return to competition. It's the end of April now. The first part alone puts her into June, and that's not counting her therapy. She's going to miss her entire rodeo circuit and I can't help but feel like it's our fault."

Shannon's sadness made Carter's heart squeeze. He couldn't hold himself back from tucking some of her hair behind her ear. She brought her hand up and placed it over his to cup the side of her face. "Rhett said it's an accident and accidents are part of life."

"Your brother's right," Carter said.

She gave a sad smile. "How's Hawken?"

Carter slipped his hand away from her face, and then he turned to the side, shoving the same hand into his hair. "It's hard to tell without being able to review his full medical history, but Spira and I both think he has a muscle strain as well as possible moderate damage to the tendon on the same leg." He crossed to the stall Hawken was being kept in and used two fingers to brush the palomino's mane from his forehead. "Even if Violet was fine, Hawken's got at least three months until he can start training again, but that's only if he didn't hurt a tendon. If he's hurt a tendon, then we're looking at nine to twelve months."

Shannon came up beside him in front of the stall. "A year? She won't be able to use him for that long? That'll ruin her career."

Carter rested his forearms on the edge of the stall door, his shoulders slumping. "If she cares about her horse more than winning awards and cash prizes, she'll do what's best for him."

"Carter." Shannon touched his arm. He straightened as he turned to face her and she was so close. Only a breath away. And she was looking up at him with so much hope in her eyes it made his heart come to a full stop. Her eyes searched his as she bit her bottom lip. "I didn't come here to talk about horses," she whispered as her hands found his chest.

She was so beautiful and so kind and caring and he couldn't be with her. It was killing him. She deserved a guy who was upright and from a good family. She needed someone who could seamlessly meld with her family—and that wasn't him. If Amy was right, it would never be him.

"Shannon, I—"

She inched closer. "I love you, Carter. I should have told you the other day. I should have told you the second I started to fall for you, but I can't quite put my finger on when that was. Because the truth is it feels like a piece of my heart has always been waiting for you."

Before he could respond she went up on her tiptoes and her lips found his. For half a second Carter considered breaking the kiss. Given his scattered thoughts, that would have been the responsible thing to do. But with Shannon's arms around him and her mouth melding with his, he couldn't think beyond the moment. Beyond kissing her one last time.

If it was their last kiss, then he was going to make

it count. Carter pressed his hand to the small of her back, making it so there was no space between them. Then he—

The door behind them swung open, and the sound snapped Carter back to his senses before he could deepen the kiss or draw his hands into her hair. Shannon and Carter sprang apart.

Wade came to a stumbling halt a few feet away. "You didn't answer your phone."

Shannon's glare was sharp enough to draw blood. "Maybe because my phone was on silent and I was a little busy, if you hadn't noticed."

"We need you in the house." He grabbed for his sister's arm. "Now."

She jerked away from him. "Are you purposely trying to keep Carter and me apart? We talked about this, Wade. It seems a little convenient that you need me *every time* we start kissing." She crossed her arms. "If this is some big ploy then—"

Wade yanked on his hair and growled, "June's dead, Shannon. She's dead."

"What?" Shannon's knees crumpled and she would have hit the barn's cement floor if Carter hadn't surged forward and caught her. She leaned heavily into Carter as she dashed a tear away. "You're sure?"

Wade nodded. "We just got off with Boone."

"How?" A sob burst from her mouth. Carter held her more securely against his chest.

Wade glanced at Carter and then back to Shannon. "She was on that hiking trip with some ladies from her church. They were taking a group picture near a ledge."

Wade's voice hitched. "She fell." He pinched the bridge of his nose. "It was a three-hundred-foot sheer drop to the rocks." He closed his eyes as he wrapped his hand over his mouth.

Shannon trembled in Carter's arms and then she unwound herself and stumbled toward her brother. Wade pulled her into a hug and they both started crying together. Carter stepped backward until he was against the wall. It felt as if he shouldn't be here, shouldn't bear witness to this moment of their deep, private pain.

"We have to go up to the house." Wade set Shannon back a little from himself. "Boone asked that we handle all funeral arrangements. He's got his hands full with Hailey, but they're trying to get on the first plane here so they can be with us. He wants the funeral here, of course, since all their family lives near." Wade guided Shannon out of the barn and neither gave a backward glance to Carter.

Carter had never felt more like an outsider, like he didn't belong, than he did right now.

Chapter Twelve

A day later, the second Boone had made it through the door of Rhett's house, Shannon threw her arms around him. "I'm so sorry. We all loved her so much." Her tears were immediate and overwhelming. Boone's arms came around her as they cried together.

While Boone and his family had lived out of state for the last few years, he and June were both locals. They had been high school sweethearts at Stillwater High. Shannon had known and loved June long before she was officially her sister-in-law, and Boone and June had lived at Red Dog Ranch for the first few years of their marriage. Early on, everyone had teased the couple because their names had rhymed and there had been all sorts of jovial speculation about what they would name their daughter when June was pregnant with Hailey.

And now June was gone. That quickly.

Just like their dad.

Life could change so drastically, so fast.

Boone's breathing hitched and his shoulders shud-

dered as she hugged him, and that made Shannon cry
even harder. Her brother was a rock of a man—he had
arms like a bodybuilder yet he was incredibly book
smart. Shannon loved all her brothers for different reasons. She knew she could go to Rhett with anything
and he would help her. Wade had always been her best
friend and also her confidant in mischief, and Boone
had been an anchor for her. Steady, dependable and
levelheaded. A unique blend of reasoning mixed with
compassion. It tore her in two to see her big, strong
brother so broken-down.

Boone let go of Shannon and moved on to the next
person. Wade had gone to the airport to pick up Boone
and Hailey while the rest of the family had assembled
at Rhett's to put final touches on the funeral that would
take place on Wednesday. Wade walked into the house
behind Boone, holding Hailey in one arm and Piper in
the other. Cassidy went to Wade and placed her hand
on his back as she greeted Hailey and kissed Piper on
the cheek. Boone moved down the line, hugging Rhett,
Macy and then their mother, who held on to him as if
he might disappear if she let go.

As Hailey watched the scene, she suddenly burst into
loud, uncontrollable tears. "I. Want. My. Mom." Her tiny
shoulders trembled with each sob. "I miss my mom,"
she wailed. Boone snatched her away from Wade and
headed upstairs without a word. A few people sniffled,
but other than that they stood there in silence, listening to Hailey's wild, mournful cries filling the house.

Kodiak lifted her head and let out a long, low whine.
Shannon bowed her head. *Lord, I don't know how*

*to make this better. I don't know how to help. Please,
be here with us. Let us feel You here, even in this really hard stuff. Especially in this hard stuff. Be with
Boone and Hailey.*

Rhett braced his hand on the kitchen counter. "We
are going to see and feel a lot of pain for a while. But
this is what family does." He tucked Macy close to his
side. "Yes, we enjoy the good times together, but the
important thing is we're here for each other when times
are the hardest. I don't know how Boone and Hailey
will deal with this, but I do know we're going to be
with them every step of the way."

Shannon nodded along. She had never loved her family more.

Shannon hadn't seen Carter since Saturday after the
horse show, so by Tuesday afternoon she ended up seeking him out. She didn't blame him for not coming to
find her on Sunday or Monday—she had been busy with
her family. But now she wanted someone she could go to
with her grief. She wanted someone to be there for her
because she felt completely drained and wrung out and
knew it would only be harder tomorrow at the funeral.

She wanted Carter.

She found him mucking out the stall Hawken had
been using. He had moved Hawken to the one next
door, and the palomino, along with Carter's ever-present
goose surveyor in the hallway, watched the man's every
move.

"Hey, you." Shannon came up to the open doorway.

Carter leaned on the rake he had been using to spread

the fresh straw. His gaze slowly appraised her. "How are you doing with everything?"

"Not great." She knit her fingers together. "It's really sad and it's really hard. I know that's not super eloquent, but I don't have the reserves for eloquence right now. It's just so incredibly sad." She looked down at her entwined fingers. "Nothing I say to Boone is going to help and Hailey is a mess."

Carter's smile was sad but encouraging. "It'll take a long time before things feel normal. And honestly, life will probably never be normal for them again. But they just need you around, Shannon. That's the best thing you can do."

She loved that Carter's advice always seemed to be a balance of truth and compassion. She gave him a watery smile. "I've really missed you."

He returned a sad smile but made no move toward her.

Why hadn't Carter put the rake down? They were five feet apart. She just needed him to bridge five feet and hold her. Was that too much to ask?

She swiped at her eyes. "So the funeral is tomorrow at eleven. The ceremony is, of course, being held here at the ranch's chapel." She dug into her front pocket for one of the tissues she had stashed there earlier. "There will be a seat for you up in front by me."

"I—ah." Carter rubbed at his jaw, looked away. "I can't sit up front with your family."

"Of course you can." Shannon felt as if she couldn't fill her lungs completely with air no matter how hard she tried. "I need you there, Carter."

Leaning the rake against the wall, he held up a hand

in a gesture that could only be interpreted as *stay back*. "I didn't know June Jarrett and I've never met Boone. It feels...wrong...to have a front-row seat to something so intimate."

There was a painful tightening in the back of her throat. Why was he making this difficult? Why couldn't he just be there for her like she needed him to be? "You wouldn't be sitting up there for them. You'd be there for me." She pressed her hands to her chest.

He edged around her into the hallway. "I can't."

She reached for him, but her reaction time was too slow and her hand only grabbed air. "I need you, Carter. This is really hard. I need you there."

Carter's lips pressed together, forming a slight grimace. "You don't need me. You never have."

"I do."

The muscle that ran along his jaw ticked once, twice. He folded his arms over his chest. "I didn't even attend my own mother's funeral, Shannon. I'm not attending this one, either."

Shannon laid a hand on the outer wall of the stall for support. "I thought..." She looked up, searching to meet Carter's eyes but he kept his head down. "But as my boyfriend..."

His eyes closed and he sighed deeply as he rubbed his forehead. "I'm not your boyfriend. We never—I'm not your boyfriend."

Every hug, every kiss, every deep conversation flashed through her mind. Sure, they hadn't said the words...but they had been acting like a couple for a while now. She had told him she loved him.

Indignation and a dash of humiliation rose up, burning her throat, making it feel raw. "Oh, so you just make out with girls and then don't date them. Is that it?"

At least he had the decency to flinch.

"Why are you acting like this?" Shannon took a few cautious steps closer. "This isn't you. This isn't how you've been the whole time we've known each other."

He finally met her gaze and his eyes were empty of emotion; looking into them caused a chill to race down her back. She had once compared his eyes to a welcoming ocean that beckoned her to dive in, but no longer. No, they were the dark waters of nighttime sailing, with dangers lurking under the stillness. What was going on in his mind? What had caused him to act like this? She wished he would tell her.

"We've known each other a month, Shannon," he said. "It's been a good month, but I—I've got to get out of here." He shoved his hand into his hair and pivoted away. "I'm not the boyfriend type and I'm certainly not the family type that goes to funerals." He threw out a hand. "Besides, you don't need me. You're strong, Shannon. I've been saying that all along. You don't need anyone to hold you up."

A sense of betrayal shattered through her. Carter didn't want her. He wanted to cut his losses and run. It had been foolish to believe that he would somehow change the pattern he had followed for the last thirteen years just because of her. Hadn't she promised herself she wouldn't be led by her emotions any longer?

This was why. The pain. The sense of something vital being torn from her insides.

Love wasn't worth this.

Tears blasted down her cheeks, but she didn't bother to wipe them away. Shannon forced all the muscles in her body to tense as she marched up to Carter and said, "Being strong doesn't negate needing other people. Actually, I think it's the opposite. I think strong people are the ones who can admit they need others, that they can't handle life on their own. But you? You just run away whenever life gets difficult or sticky. All you know how to do is walk away and then you make yourself feel better by telling yourself that you're somehow strong because you're all alone in life. But the truth is you're weak, Carter. You're a coward who only knows how to tuck your tail and run."

His nostrils widened as he worked his jaw back and forth. "Well, at least there's something we agree on." He brushed past her, getting out of the cornered situation she had him in. "If you don't mind, I need to get out of here. I'm so good at running away, after all. I'm sorry I wasted your time these last few weeks." He shoved through the door that led outside.

Shannon followed on his heels, wanting to apologize instantly but also feeling far too drained to chase after him. Besides, he owed her an apology, too.

All she saw was his back and as she grabbed the doorjamb to keep her feet, she wondered if this image of Carter's strong shoulders getting smaller and smaller would be the last of him she would ever see. But after his words, she *shouldn't* care. She wouldn't care.

There were more important things going on in her life than a broken heart.

* * *

More than likely, Carter should have turned his truck right toward the city limits and driven as far as his tank of gas would take him. He should have packed his things and headed for the state line and never looked back.

He should have done a lot of things that he hadn't.

As if on autopilot, he drove straight to the Spiras'. Over the past few weeks their home had become a sort of safe haven for him. When he arrived, he tossed his truck into Park and yanked the keys out of the ignition. Then, gripping the wheel tightly, he pressed his forehead against it and let out a loud yell.

Saying those things...walking away from Shannon Jarrett had been the most difficult thing he had ever done in his life. And Carter had done his share of difficult things. *It's for the best. It's for her best.* Maybe if he kept repeating that, it might stop feeling as if he had left half of himself at Red Dog Ranch.

But he wasn't holding his breath.

A light tap against his window made him lift his head. Mrs. Spira beamed at him as if his face wasn't streaked red from the tears he had shed during his drive over and he hadn't just been hollering in her driveway.

With green-gloved hands, she lofted a large metal watering can. "I could use your strong, young back if you're actually planning to get out of that thing you call a truck." She spoke loudly to be heard through his closed door.

Carter scrubbed his hand down his face, took a deep breath and headed outside.

Her lips skewed to the side as she squinted at him.

"Let me guess." She wagged her finger. "You went and did something really stupid."

He exhaled a harsh puff of air. "Stupid? Yes. Necessary? Unfortunately, also, yes."

She foisted the watering can into his hands and waved for him to follow her. "Keep up now." She brought him to the lush backyard and directed him to water a little tree. "That one's doing all right." She walked over to another potted tree, which was limp and discolored. She ran a finger over the tiny trunk. "This is one of the branches I'm trying to grow a tree from but it's not taking correctly. I feel as if I've done everything right but the roots aren't growing." She huffed. "All the waiting can be beyond frustrating."

Mrs. Spira tugged off one of her gardening gloves so she could reach inside the oversize pockets on the apron she wore. She pulled a packet of Miracle-Gro out and poured it into the watering can.

"I think it just needs the right food, is all. And some more time." She eased the watering can from his hands and sprinkled the mixture over the potted branch. "I'm not ready to give up on it quite yet." Using the back of her hand, she lightly smacked his shoulder. "Some people would give up on it, you know. They'd toss it away, never knowing what a beautiful tree it could become." She headed to the next patch of growth and used the watering can there. Then, without looking at him, she said, "You had a row with your lady, didn't you?"

"She's not *my* lady." And if she ever had been, she certainly wasn't anymore after how he had acted.

Mrs. Spira laughed loudly. "My right eye she's not."

"It's complicated."

"Oh, Carter, *life* is complicated. Be happy for that. If it's not complicated it's because you've died." She popped a hand to her hip. "We face struggles of all kinds from the day we're born until that last breath. So don't feed me *it's complicated*."

Carter felt his lips twitching with a smile. "Has anyone ever told you that you don't hold back?"

She batted her hand in the air. "Life's too short to be agreeable." She set the watering can down next to a sawed-off tree stump and pointed toward a small metal table and chair set nearby. Once they were seated, she slapped her gloves onto the table. "Well, out with it. What did you do?"

"I left Red Dog Ranch," he said. "For good."

She nodded along as if she had expected as much. "And why would you go and do a thing like that?"

"Because I can't stay at that ranch and not be in love with Shannon at the same time." He splayed his hands on the table. "It's not physically possible." He thought back to Saturday in the barn after the horse show. "I tried to pull back, to just be a coworker, but we ended up kissing again."

Mrs. Spira leaned her chin on her fist and smiled as widely as the Cheshire cat.

"So I had to push her away," Carter said. "I'm not the tied-down kind of guy. I don't want people counting on me when I know I'm only going to end up letting them down eventually. I always do, even when I try not to." The words felt gummy and wrong in his mouth but he said them anyway. "She wanted me to sit beside her at June Jarrett's funeral—up front."

Mrs. Spira looked on thoughtfully but didn't open her mouth. Odd.

So Carter rambled on. "When I came here, the plan was to save money, learn and get out. I was never supposed to become entrenched enough with anyone to be expected to sit in the front row at a funeral."

"Oh, my." She folded her hands on the table and her shoulders rose with a long inhale. "Now, I'm not a doctor, but it sounds to me like you have a very serious condition."

A tingle of worry skated down his back. "Condition?"

"Indeed." She nodded solemnly. "It sounds as if you have a very serious condition called *being human*." Mrs. Spira frowned. "I'm sorry to tell you, but it's incurable. And because of it you will make mistakes until the day you die." Her eyes grew wide as she stage-whispered, "I have it, too."

Where had the Spiras been his whole life? If they had been in his life earlier, Carter could have been saved from so many troubles and mistakes.

Carter heaved a sigh. "So at least I'm in good company."

"Have you ever heard about the parable of the sowers?" Mrs. Spira asked. "It's in the Bible."

"Of course," he said, but then he wasn't completely sure, so he followed that up with the gist of what he remembered. "It's the one where some seeds were thrown onto rocks and other seeds went into soil. The ones on the rocks never grew, and some in parts of the soil grew but they were choked by weeds, and some flourished."

Mrs. Spira looked as if she wanted to hand him a gold star sticker. "Great summary," she said. "Now, what does it tell you about the different types of soil?"

He shrugged. "I guess that you need good soil and no weeds to have the best chance at growing something."

"At growing *you*, son." She pointed at him. "I know you believe in God, Carter. But I wonder if you know what it means to walk with Him. Because despite loving God, your tree hasn't grown roots and isn't flourishing."

And there it was. He had finally managed to disappoint Mrs. Spira.

Carter's jaw went rigid.

She must have sensed him pulling away, though, because she quickly snaked her hand across the table and took one of his hands. "Plants need food and water and sunshine to grow, Carter. If we don't give them those things, they'll die even when they're planted in the very best soil." Her thumb rubbed over the back of his hand. "Do you know how we water ourselves—in a religious sense? We pray, Carter. We spend time with other people who love God. We talk about God and worship Him." She tugged his hand across the table so he couldn't get away. "When you thought through all those reasons to not be with Shannon, did you pray about it? Did you ask God about your relationship with Shannon? Or have you only been directed by your own heart and mind—which, need I remind you, are affected by your...condition?"

Carter swallowed hard. "I didn't pray about it." He

swallowed again, feeling foolish. "If I'm being honest, I don't pray very much at all."

"Yet you think you know what's best in the situation? You think you know what's best for her? All that without getting counsel from the One who wants the best for both of you?" She clucked her tongue. "Do you see what I'm getting at?"

Mrs. Spira had been right to call him out. Carter was so used to being on his own and all his choices only affecting him, that somewhere along the road he had forgotten that God was with him. That God cared and wanted to be a part of his decision-making. That God had a good and perfect plan for the world and that included him.

More than a decade had passed since he had prayed that first time, asking God to save him, but his prayers had been few and far between since then. How could he claim a relationship if he never talked to God? It was no different than thinking he and Amy could just pick up as siblings after going for so long without being in each other's lives.

He swallowed around the Texas-size lump in his throat. "What have I done?" His voice was a croaky whisper. "How could I let this happen?"

Shannon might never want to see him after their argument. She was in the midst of mourning her sister-in-law and he had only made things worse for her. He should have held her and been there for her; instead he had left her alone and crying. Carter dropped his head into his hand. He probably didn't deserve another chance with her.

Mrs. Spira jiggled the hand she still gripped. "Get your heart right with God first. Focus on that and the rest will come to pass. Perhaps too much damage has been done with the Jarretts—for now that's not something you can control." She pressed up to her feet and rounded to where he was sitting. "But the most important thing is your relationship with God. Wrestle with Him. Pray. Do whatever you need to do to get back on the right path." She pressed a kiss to his temple. "God never gives up on His children, and I'm not quite ready to give up on you, either." She winked. "I still believe you're going to grow a beautiful family tree. I think it's all there, you just need the right nourishment first." She squeezed his shoulder and then headed back to the front of the house, leaving Carter alone at the tiny table to ponder her words.

Well, not alone.

Carter bowed his head, closed his eyes and prayed for the first time in a very long time.

Chapter Thirteen

Shannon tested the door to the ranch's office and found it unlocked. She knew Macy had been attempting to keep up with everything, but since the funeral, Hailey had attached herself to Macy so Shannon's sister-in-law hadn't been able to accomplish as much as she normally would have. Taking care of Hailey was the most important thing right now. Besides, Macy was more than eight months pregnant, so it was high time for the rest of them to start managing the responsibilities in the office.

After clearing off a large table, Shannon lugged a crate full of mail from the front room and dumped it onto the table so she could sort through correspondence. Some items, like bills and donations, required immediate attention while others could wait. It was amazing how much mail could pile up in a couple of days.

But the act of going through the letters piece by piece helped take her mind off everything, so she embraced the task. Wade and Cassidy had helped Shannon run the egg hunt that morning and afterward they had headed to their home. Shannon hadn't wanted to go up to Rhett's but she also hadn't wanted to be alone in her own home. She had offered to help Cassidy start prepping food for Easter dinner tomorrow, but Cassidy had turned her down, saying Wade would be helping her and two people in the kitchen was enough.

Shannon felt a little guilty that she needed a break from the grieving, but Rhett and Macy were with Boone and Hailey right now and they wouldn't miss her for a few hours.

When Wing Cosby had almost died, Shannon had thought she wouldn't be able to survive another loss. But June was gone. They had been left with no choice but to accept the loss and deal with it. She was crushed to lose her sister-in-law, but at the same time, Shannon marveled at how God had strengthened and stretched her in the past month. Just like Rhett had said at the house, this pain wouldn't break their family, it would only make them stronger.

She lifted a large manila envelope from the pile and froze. It was addressed to Carter Kelly. The return address listed the veterinarian mission organization he had applied to.

Her throat seized up.

How had she been so wrong about him? After he left, Shannon had known what real heartbreak was. With Cord, it hadn't been this way. She hadn't felt hollowed out and raw after breaking up with him—she had only known relief. Now she knew that she had never loved Cord or any man romantically before. How she felt about Carter—she had never felt like that about anyone else.

And despite everything that had occurred, she loved Carter Kelly. Loved him completely.

Too bad it hurt so much.

At the funeral she had left the seat next to her open, waiting, hoping Carter would reconsider. Even until the end, she had held on to the hope that he would slip into the service, take the seat beside her and lift her hand into his. Just be there. That he would show up and everything would be all right. They would go back to how they had been. The other day would have been a weird blip in the course of their relationship, nothing more.

But he hadn't shown up. Not then, and not since.

Dr. Spira had been stopping by daily to check on Hawken and he had mentioned to Easton that Carter was staying at their house in town. That bit of knowledge shouldn't have made Shannon breathe easier, but it had. Days ago when he left, Shannon had worried she would never see him again. She had figured he would be in a different state, starting a new life. But for now he had decided to stay in Stillwater, Texas, and she had to wonder why.

A tiny seed in her heart couldn't help but hope it had something to do with her.

Shannon set the envelope down and sighed. She trailed her fingers over his name. If he had been around the last few days, she would have been tempted to spend time with him. She definitely wouldn't have spent as much time with Boone and Hailey. Shame lanced through her, but she knew it was true. When Carter was near, she was drawn to him. She probably wouldn't have been able to resist seeking him out, especially if they had made things official. She might have even sought him out for the very purpose of getting lost in his kisses, using him as a means to not deal with the swirl of emotions wrecking their way through her as she grieved. And doing that would have not only prolonged dealing with the grieving process, it wouldn't have been a fair way to treat Carter or a good foundation for the beginning of a relationship.

So while it hurt that Carter hadn't been there for her when she had needed him most, she forgave him.

The front door to the office area creaked open. She looked up, spotting Rhett. "Hey," she said. "What are you doing here?"

He jerked his chin toward the pile of mail. "I was going to sort through that, but it looks like you beat me to the task." Rhett lowered himself into a chair across from her. "I really appreciate all you've been doing this week to keep the place running."

She pulled her legs up onto her chair and gathered her arms around them. "It's nice to feel useful for once."

"For once?" His eyebrows shot up.

"You know how it is," she said. "You and Macy run the place. Cassidy keeps us all fed. As head of maintenance, Wade keeps all the equipment and buildings in working condition. Everyone has a role." She lifted one shoulder in a half-hearted shrug. "Everyone but me."

"Shannon, look at me." Rhett's voice was soft and warm. "It was *you* who kept the ranch running when I didn't live here, Boone went to school and we thought

Wade was dead. It was *you* who held this family together and took care of Mom all by yourself after Dad
died. *You* were the one holding our parents' hands at the
hospital when they found out about Mom's Alzheimer's
diagnosis. You have done more for this family and the
ranch in the last few years than the rest of us combined.
Without you, Red Dog Ranch wouldn't be here today."

"Do you really…" Tears clouded her vision and her
throat suddenly felt too tight. "Do you mean that?"

"You know I'm not one to just say things." He leaned
forward in his chair, his arms resting on the table. "I'm
sorry how we acted made you doubt your worth here
and I'm sorry you weren't aware of how much we appreciate and value all you've done for the family and
for the ranch. If I'd known you felt this way, I would
have made sure you knew the truth. I'll do better from
now on. In a week or two, let's sit down and carve out
a defined position for you here."

"I'd really like to help with training our staff members who work with the children and would love to
oversee some of that. And I'd also love to expand the
horsemanship program into something much bigger."

He nodded. "That seems like a good fit."

As he talked, she had set her feet back on the ground
and laid her hands on top of Carter's envelope. She
fiddled with one of the corners, curling it up and then
pressing it firmly back down.

Rhett twisted his head in an effort to read the envelope. "What have you got there?"

"Mail addressed to Carter." She smoothed a finger

over the lettering. "Looks like it might be the response from the mission organization he applied to."

A tilted grin made her big brother look adorable. "Are you going to bring it to him?"

"Should I?"

Rhett shrugged. "He deserves to know. Though we could always forward it or give it to Spira next time he stops by. He's here often enough."

Shannon's hopes plummeted. "Oh, right."

"Or—" Rhett tapped the envelope "—you could bring it to him and invite him to Easter dinner."

"And just why would I do that?"

"Because you're in love with him, Shannon." Rhett's smile was huge. "Because guys can be incredibly hard-headed and he may wish everything had ended differently but doesn't know how to make it right. When Macy and I had our falling out—we lost so many years we could have been together because I was stubborn and thought she was better-off without me. Look at Wade. He loved Cassidy and somehow convinced himself that abandoning her for five years was the most loving thing he could do." Rhett closed his eyes and shook his head. "Both of us were total blockheads who are incredibly blessed our wives fought for our relationships and kept pushing us." Rhett grimaced. "I'm afraid Carter may have the same blockhead gene. It tends to be a dominant trait in the males of our species."

Could it be that simple? If she saw Carter, could they repair the damage they had both created and move forward? Rhett and Macy had. Wade and Cassidy had, too. Why *not* her?

There was only one way to find out.

Shannon hugged the envelope to her chest. "He deserves to know as soon as possible, right?"

Rhett got up and unhooked one of the many keys from the wall. Shannon had never needed to own her own car because the ranch had a slew of vehicles dedicated to staff use. The keys hung on the pegboard in the office where staff members signed them out whenever they took one. "Take the Jeep." Rhett dangled the key from his hand. "It's got a full tank of gas and Wade finished all the tune-ups on it yesterday."

She took the keys from his hand and then leaned in, hugging him. "I love you, Rhett. Thanks for being a great big brother."

He kissed her on the cheek. "It's easy when I have the best sister out there."

She gave him another squeeze and then headed out. She would figure out what to say to Carter along the way.

Carter was putting together a shelving unit for Mrs. Spira when the doorbell rang.

"I'll get it," Dr. Spira called from the other room. A few seconds later he poked his head into the study where Carter and Mrs. Spira were working. "It's for you, son."

Carter dusted his hands on his jeans and headed toward the front room. When he turned the corner and saw Shannon waiting there, his heart stuttered along with his voice. "Wh-what are you—you're here."

"This came for you." She held out a large envelope. "It's from the mission."

He glanced at it and then up at her. With everything else going on, he had forgotten he had even applied. Carter licked his lips.

She jiggled the envelope until he finally took it from her hands.

"Well," she said. "What are you waiting for? Open it."

But he was having a hard time processing beyond the fact that she was here. Shannon was three feet away and she wasn't glaring at him or crying or telling him to get out of town. Ever since his conversation with Mrs. Spira, Carter had been praying for Shannon and praying that they would have an opportunity to reconcile. But he hadn't wanted to crowd her by showing up at the ranch, especially not when her family was in the middle of dealing with a tragedy.

Carter set the envelope on the table and took a cautious step in her direction. "I'm sorry, Shannon. I was a jerk about the funeral—I should have been there for you and done whatever you needed." His words spilled out quickly. "I—I failed you. Leaving Red Dog Ranch, leaving you." His next step brought them only a foot apart.

The soft, warm expression she wore said it was okay to proceed, so he did. "I've never regretted something more in my life. I'll never be able to make it up to you, but I'd like to try if you're willing to let me come home. And I don't mean Red Dog Ranch." He lifted a tentative hand to her face to tuck a curl behind her ear.

"I mean you, Shannon. Being around you—that's the most at-home I've ever felt in my whole life." He met her unwavering eye contact. "I love you."

"I love you, too, Carter," she whispered. "I said some horrible things to you. I'm so sorry I called you a coward. You're not. With everything you've been through in your life, you're incredibly brave."

"I forgive you," he said. "Will you forgive me?"

Then her lips parted into a teasing grin that did all sorts of funny things to his insides. "I'll forgive you under one condition."

He quirked an eyebrow. "Which is?"

She looked up at him through hooded eyes. "Kiss me."

"Gladly." He gathered her in his arms and found her lips. Found home. Her fingers found the sides of his face and trailed back to touch the hair at the base of his neck. Carter groaned and adjusted his mouth as he pulled her tighter against his chest.

A loud whoop behind him caused them to break apart. The Spiras had entered the room at some point and were cheering, their arms around each other.

Shannon blushed and buried her face in Carter's chest. He wrapped his arms around her and kissed the top of her head. "I told you about Audrey. She's the only person I ever dated. I've never been in a real relationship before." He laid his cheek on top of her head. "Not like this, not where I was head over heels gone on someone. And I don't know if I'll do everything right."

Shannon pushed on his chest, setting herself back

to look into his eyes. "We can make this work as long as we keep being honest with each other."

Carter nodded. Shannon was right; it was time to start being completely honest with each other. "The day of the horse show I got a call from my sister. She implied I may not be fit to be a part of a family." His fingertips found her hair again. "That's why I pulled away."

"I'm so sorry, Carter," she said. "I know how much you want to reconcile with her. We'll keep praying about it together, okay?"

He swallowed hard. "I promise not to keep stuff like that from you from now on. We both know I've done a lot wrong so far, but if you'll have me, I'd like to try." He offered a tentative smile as she dashed a tear from her cheek.

"And I promise I'll pray more and keep working on myself." He glanced back at the Spiras. "Mrs. Spira helped me see that was part of what has been getting me into trouble for so long."

Shannon hugged his middle. "I promise to pray more and keep working on myself, too. But I want to be with you, Carter. I want to be together." Shannon slipped away from him and picked the envelope back up. "I think it's time to open this."

Carter fumbled to tear it open but finally did. He pulled out the packet inside. *"Welcome to..."* "I got in." He handed Shannon the letter. "They want me to be part of the South America trip this summer."

Shannon squealed, jumped up and down and then hugged him again. "I'm so proud of you."

"I'm not going to take it." He tugged the letter from

her grasp and let it fall to the floor. Then he took both of her hands into his. "For the first time in my life I have a reason to stay. I want to be with you and if that means passing up a hundred opportunities like this, I will."

"But it's your dream." She squeezed his hand at the word *dream*. "I'll wait for you. It's only three months. I would miss you, but I'll be right here when you get back."

"It might have been, but dreams change," he said. "I've changed."

Dr. Spira cleared his throat. "I'm sorry to barge in, but I have two bits of information that might help." He held up two fingers. "The first is that particular mission allows spouses to go along and, being a member of the board of the organization, I happen to know they still have room on that trip for extras."

Carter's mouth dropped open. He hadn't known Spira was on the board—that was shocking enough— but had the man just suggested Shannon and Carter get married?

The Spiras both smiled and nodded encouragingly.

Carter moistened his lips and turned back to Shannon. "I'm not going to lie and say I haven't already thought about marriage," Carter said. "I want that with you and I'm already in my thirties, so I don't want to wait too long." He scrubbed at the back of his neck. "But…I'm forehead-deep in debt from my school loans, and if I go on this trip that's three months without pay, which sets us three months back from even the hope of one day being in the spot where I have enough saved for us to be comfortably married and—"

Spira coughed. "Which brings me to my second point." The doctor held up a finger. "I always dreamed I'd leave my practice to one of my children one day, but they went and had the audacity to have dreams of their own, none of which included becoming a veterinarian. But then God brought me you." He wrapped an arm around his wife.

"And we think of you like our son," Mrs. Spira said. "You're family to us now."

Carter's knees went weak at their declaration. He latched onto Shannon for support. Shannon wrapped an arm around his middle and squeezed him to her side.

"So when you return from the mission, I'd like to give you my practice," Dr. Spira said. "Free of charge, of course. That way you don't have to worry about the expense of starting one from scratch. My practice may seem on the small side, but I can tell you, it does rather well."

Carter sank to sit on the coffee table. "I don't know what to say."

"I'll stay on for a year and advise you, of course. But then after that—" he looked at his wife and they shared a loving look "—after that we're going to move to Galveston to be near our grandchildren."

"I can't accept this. It's too much."

Spira left the room for a minute and returned with a file folder in his hands. "Too bad," he said, "I already started the legal process to change the ownership. I just need your signature." He walked forward, holding out the folder. "I built this practice to be an inheritance, son. I never wanted to sell it."

Carter stood, but he ignored the folder and pulled the doctor into a hug instead. They had called him a member of their family. They had called him *son*. Carter reached out to Shannon and pulled her into their hug, too, and then he held out an arm, inviting Mrs. Spira into the embrace. She readily joined. The four of them stood there holding each other for a few minutes before they broke apart, everyone swiping at their eyes.

"Would you all like to join us for Easter dinner tomorrow?" Shannon asked. Everyone agreed they wouldn't miss it.

Carter headed back to the guest bedroom to pack his things. As he slung the duffel holding his meager possessions onto his back, he couldn't help but feel as if he was the richest man in the world. He had Shannon's love, the Spiras' acceptance and he had God's guidance. Nothing else mattered in the world.

After he said goodbye to the Spiras, he headed outside with Shannon. She reached for his hand. "Let's go home."

He dropped his duffel bag on the ground so he could pull her to his chest unhindered. "You're here, Shannon." He drank in her gaze and the beautiful trust and vulnerability radiating from her smile. "That means I'm already home." Then he brought his lips to hers and gave her a kiss that spoke of all the promises and dreams they would share together.

* * * * *

*Be sure to watch for Boone's story,
coming later this year!*

Dear Reader,

The statistics aren't pretty. One in three women will experience domestic violence at some point in their life-time, and one in ten children is a victim of or witnesses domestic violence in their homes. If that's you, know that you are worthy of love and it grieves the heart of God to see you mistreated. When you're ready, please call the National Domestic Violence Hotline.

Carter and Shannon both deal with a lot of really tough things and I was so excited when they reached a happy ending. Make sure to look up the rest of the books in the Red Dog Ranch series. Each sibling gets their own story! Please connect with me on my Facebook author page and remember—book reviews are always greatly appreciated.

Thank you for reading!
Jessica Keller

COMING NEXT MONTH FROM
Love Inspired

Available February 18, 2020

THE AMISH TEACHER'S DILEMMA
North Country Amish • by Patricia Davids
Taking a schoolteacher position in another district was just the change Amish spinster Eva Coblentz needed. But with her family insisting she come home just as she falls for three troubled orphans and their guardian uncle, Willis Gingrich, will she return to her old life...or risk everything to build a new one?

HEALING THEIR AMISH HEARTS
Colorado Amish Courtships • by Leigh Bale
Becca Graber has made it her mission to get the silent boy in her new classroom to speak again. But she's not quite sure *why* he doesn't talk. Working with the child's father, widower Jesse King, can she break through to little Sam...and begin to repair all their broken hearts?

FINDING THE ROAD HOME
Hearts of Oklahoma • by Tina Radcliffe
With potential budget cuts looming, police chief Mitch Rainbolt may have to let his latest hire go—unless he and officer Daisy Anderson can prove that their department deserves the money. Can they save her job...and ensure Daisy and her orphaned nieces and nephews stay in town for good?

THE TEXAN'S PROMISE
Cowboys of Diamondback Ranch • by Jolene Navarro
To save her ranch, Belle De La Rosa must sell part of it to developers—and only conservationist Quinn Sinclair stands in her way. Belle can't help but feel drawn to the widower and his children, but will she take a chance on love even when she finds out his true reason for being in town?

THE COWBOY'S UNEXPECTED BABY
Triple Creek Cowboys • by Stephanie Dees
When rancher and attorney Garrett Cole finds a newborn baby on his doorstep, he has no idea how to even change a diaper. Help comes in the form of Abby Scott, his new temporary coworker. But can Garrett convince Abby she'd be the perfect permanent addition to his makeshift family?

HER SECRET TWINS
by Janette Foreman
Kallie Shore's late father knew she couldn't raise her girls *and* work the family farm alone. But the plan he specified in his will isn't the one she'd have chosen: Kallie inherits half the farm, but the other half goes to Grant Young, her ex-fiancé...and the secret father of her twins.

Clang, clang, clang.

The hammering outside her new schoolhouse grew louder. Eva Coblentz moved to the window to locate the source of the clatter. Across the road she saw a man pounding on an ancient-looking piece of machinery with steel wheels and a scoop-like nose on the front end.

When he had the sheet of metal shaped to fit the front of the machine, he stood back to assess his work. He knelt and hammered on the shovel-like nose three more times. Satisfied, he gathered up his tools and started in her direction.

She stepped back from the window. Was he coming to the school? Why? Had he noticed her gawking? Perhaps he only wanted to welcome the new teacher, although his lack of a beard said he wasn't married.

She glanced around the room. Should she meet him by the door? That seemed too eager. Her eyes settled on the large desk at the front of the classroom. She should look as if she was ready for the school year to start. A professional attitude would put off any suggestion that she was interested in meeting single men.

LIEXP0220

Eva hurried to the desk, pulled out the chair and sat down as the outside door opened. The chair tipped over backward, sending her flailing. Her head hit the wall with a painful thud as she slid to the floor. Stunned, she slowly opened her eyes to see the man leaning over the desk.

He had the most beautiful gray eyes she'd ever beheld. They were rimmed with thick, dark lashes in stark contrast to the mop of curly, dark red hair springing out from beneath his straw hat. Tiny sparks of light whirled around him.

"I'm Willis Gingrich. Local blacksmith." He squatted beside her. "Can you tell me your name?"

The warmth and strength of his hand on her skin sent a sizzle of awareness along her nerve endings. "I'm Eva Coblentz. I am the new teacher and I'm fine now."

Don't miss
The Amish Teacher's Dilemma
by USA TODAY *bestselling author Patricia Davids,*
available March 2020 wherever
Love Inspired books and ebooks are sold.

LoveInspired.com